POSEIDON PRESS

NEW YORK

LONDON

TORONTO

SYDNEY

TOKYO

PHYSICAL CULTURE

A NOVEL BY

HILLARY

JOHNSON

Poseidon Press
Simon & Schuster Building
Rockefeller Center
1230 Avenue of the Americas
New York, New York 10020

Copyright © 1989 by Hillary Johnson

POSEIDON PRESS is a registered trademark
of Simon & Schuster Inc.

POSEIDON PRESS colophon is a trademark
of Simon & Schuster Inc.

Designed by Liney Li
Manufactured in the United States of America

1   3   5   7   9   10   8   6   4   2

Library of Congress Cataloging in Publication Data

Johnson, Hillary.
Physical culture : a novel / by Hillary Johnson.
p.   cm.
I. Title.
PS3560.037835P47   1989
813′.54—dc20
89-32943
CIP

ISBN 0-671-67818-3

That is not it at all,
That is not what I meant, at all.

—T. S. Eliot

SUNDAY MORNING

I'M looking at a hot dog bun, and it reminds me of a finger that has undergone a transformation and become a bad thing. Fat, dry, white, like blown-up bone cells, no fingernail, just a few incriminating crinkles in the tan skin. I'm in a black mood, I can tell, because this hot dog bun is making the muscles in my groin shrink up and send a shiver spinning off the head of my penis. It would retch if only it could figure out how.

What I feel is remorse. I wish all my extremities would fall off in remorse, the way a lizard's tail detaches when it's pinned to the ground. Extremities can't be good. They're out there wielding their own influence, susceptible to trouble, and yet: if they get caught in a bad situation, you feel them as if they were attached to the base of your spine. That's why this hot dog bun is getting to me—it looks like a big, undifferentiated appendage—it could be anything.

But I'm forty-something and haven't been able to cast off a

single organ. I've pretended to be sick till it hurts, but I haven't achieved the spontaneous corruption of flesh.

The lizard's tail is bringing to mind all kinds of dubious animals. Water-skippers, snakes, amphibious toads, turtles, and flying squirrels—they're the worst, flashing the trees with their dirty overcoats of skin, then flinging themselves on the victimized branches. Most animals fly, walk, hop, or swim, but very few can do more than one without being revolting—well, you can't have everything, I guess, without turning into a monster.

Something about the recent thought of animals is causing the inner curves of my eyeballs to grow tender, irritating the nerve that goes straight to my stomach—and I think I will be sick. I can feel the glands by my back teeth kick in very mechanically today: a hasty and perfunctory bad taste. This is the first time, in the long time I've been here, that I've felt like myself.

I should get up and comb the bushes for a good spot. The trouble ebbs, but I fold myself over the stone fence that's blocking the cars from the front yard and look around. My co-workers are milling about, but they're far enough away. I take a minute to feel the sun, committing its warmth to memory, and savor the thought of how good I'll feel just as soon as I've thrown up. My chin fits into the ball of my hand, and I hook one finger down my throat.

Nothing happens. I retch once, and right away I feel better, even though nothing comes out. This is a good thing, because throwing up really tears apart the stomach.

I hop up on the stone fence and sit down facing the lawn.

There are a lot of people here from the factory, and I know them all, although all I know about them at the moment is that they're not making mattresses. Marjorie's daughter isn't here, as far as I can tell, but I think she'll show up since Marjorie's the one who is giving the company picnic. Even after what she did to me last night, she might come. She's back at the factory again, and sometimes I see her when I pick up Marjorie for work. She might be taking a shower in the bathroom right now, water heaving on her brown, hard-wood skin.

It's not that what she did was so terrible: she punched me, that's all, in a restaurant. She was sitting by herself, as was I, and I remembered her suddenly as Marjorie's daughter. I panicked, which is what I always do when I recognize someone out of their usual context. So I went up to greet her, following through with the correct thing even when it horrifies me (that's why I'm here today).

"Hello," I said, "I'm a friend of your mother's."

She stood abruptly. "I hate my mother," she said, rounding out the last syllable of "mother" with a blow to my chin.

I watched her move in one long arc across the room until she smacked through the double glass doors with the full weight of her body and traveled past. Her date came out of the men's room, took one look at me, saw the shivering glass doors, and stalked after her.

"John!" Marjorie calls to me from the picnic table by the kitchen door. "John, come and have something to eat!"

A little bit of nausea is still oscillating at the base of my eyeballs: not bad, but as if it could stay there forever. I've just noticed the plastic cup of beer in my hand that I haven't sipped or even smelled. Reminding myself that it's 11:00 A.M., I sniff and let the glands react, then open my throat wide and keep it wide, emptying the beer over the dam of my buckled tongue, and let it flow down inconspicuously. I could drown doing this. There. I turn back to face the cars and return the beer to the cup. Anyone might think this is not a great thing to be doing.

"John!" Marjorie calls again.

I'm devastatingly obedient, forming a subversive expression as I walk, pretending it's the sunlight making me squint. I give Marjorie a raised eyebrow that turns my face into a series of disruptive, tastelessly alarming fragments—a low, relaxing chin; sharp, freckled nose that appears to be sagging slightly with age; gently billowing eyelids, above and below my eyes, smooth except for a pair of tiny, unlikely scars. The cocked eyebrow draws the corner of my jaw down toward my shoulder, my lips apart. I look parched, or faintly ill, or slightly numb around the mouth. Marjorie takes no notice of this. She has her own expressions to protect her.

"This is how you get the last of the catsup to come up the neck of the bottle," she says, squinting at me.

Her brow has grown in folds, which seem to bunch up around the bridge of her nose and hold her glasses like a fist. Ignored by all this infantile clasping, her mouth has grown slack, round and unconscionably young for her, the cheeks too.

Marjorie sidles out her feet, simulating, for a second, the legs of a folding card table, but really she doesn't have extremities. Alas, her legs are hopelessly integrated, more upholstered than lizardlike. She might pop one day, but she'll never dismember.

She plants her feet and activates her overstuffed lumps. I think they even make a gaseous wheeze as she winds up one arm. Catsup bottle in hand, she slackens her mouth further, her eyes go dim and curdled. She hurls herself into a stiff-armed pitch. I hear a grunt and step aside, although it just may be my imagination bursting in on the scene in horror.

"There," Marjorie says, jerking the catsup bottle around. She is holding the base of it in her hand. It isn't a very clean bottle she's pointing at me.

I make some new gesture with my eyebrows that means something, or could be taken to mean something, but Marjorie doesn't remove the bottle. I can't bring myself to reach out and wrap my fingers around its greasy, red neck, with its centrifugally excited engorgement of tomato paste.

"Mustard," I say.

Marjorie spreads a hot dog bun across her palm and wets it with mustard, then slides a dog inside, snuggles it in, and closes the two parts together. Wrapped in a clean white napkin, I'll take the thing into the house, along with the cup of wicked beer.

Marjorie's daughter is in Marjorie's kitchen. The cup of spit-up beer is in my hand, dangling at my side. I have very long arms, for being so short, and the beer is practically touching my knee. I've managed to slip the hot dog onto the counter, behind some canisters.

Her hair looks like the beard of a tree, as if she had fallen through her mother's roof instead of being born. If I had a gash on my leg I'd bind her hair to it, although I can't imagine her having enough patience for that. She'll never look like Marjorie, I notice. I can imagine her hair crumbling or fading, but I can't imagine an equatorial bra cutting a fold around her body.

She is staring into the open refrigerator but doesn't seem to be searching for anything, as if all she really wants to do is get away from the heat. She seems excessively calm, so I rest myself against the wall in order to watch her face. She is looking into the heart of the refrigerator, her eyes unfocused, three of her fingers sliding slowly along the thin layer of ice on the freezer compartment. Suddenly her face snaps back to attention; she smiles and grimly shakes her head, turning to me, then shuts the door decisively.

"It's too early anyway," she says, her eyes skipping off my cup for emphasis.

On the subject: I would certainly look like a fool now if I went to the sink and dumped the cup of beer as I'd planned.

"The beer's outside," I say, stepping aside to let her through the door.

I should mind my own business, but there are less than seven days left and I can afford a little curiosity. Maybe I'm just a little sentimental, too, now that I'll be leaving these lovely people so soon and don't know a thing about them.

She's still hanging around the doorway, her hair set against the cedar shake siding. That's going to hurt when she moves, I think, watching the strands settle in among the splinters. She closes her eyes to the sun. I'd like to needle her, see what happens.

"Do you know what it's like to feel your organs?" she asks, keeping her eyes closed. She raises a finger and traces imaginary organs in the air. "I know what each of mine is shaped like, where it is, and what kind of mood it's in."

This question is one I must firmly deflect in order to keep several of my own secrets intact. I think of other questions before I answer, so that my tone will be inappropriate. ("Do you know the capital of South Dakota?" "Did you pay for that, sir?")

"No," I say.

She is keeping her eyes closed for my benefit, but I can see her nether eye open a shade, as if she were squinting to see the sunlight beam on the side of her nose. Both of her eyes open now, but I know she can see only glare.

"What's it feel like?" I ask, dropping back into the conversation.

She lets her eyes rest on the lawn, rocks her head slowly, then stops. I look up at the sky and lean back on the wall, next to her.

"Distinct," she says.

"Well?"

"Well," she says, draping her hand elegantly over her abdomen and frowning, "something in here feels like a small, angry Godzilla with a huge mouth that's screaming and coughing and gnashing its gums, and spitting up big clots of blood."

She pauses.

"And the little thing has arms and it's shaking two fists and it's tearing at the corners of everything and beating the walls." She taps the tips of her fingers lightly.

She pauses again.

"It's like getting blasted in the gut with buckshot."

She watches Marjorie swing another bottle of catsup. At such a moment, she should really be wearing a look of disdain, but I recognize what she's thinking: she's in too much pain to care, as though she were used to it and less suspicious of it, in general, than of being well. She closes her eyes once more and turns back to the sun, then bends her knees and slips down the wall to the ground. The hairs snap in the cedar siding and I watch them stretch and flutter. Lazily, she smiles and crosses her ankles.

At first I'm stunned that she hasn't mentioned what she did last night, but then, seeing how tremulous her mossy head is, bowing slightly on its stem as if it were wilting in the heat, I know she's embarrassed, but she's also the most evasive creature I've ever met. She wants to distract me from the questions she knows I must have: that's the reason for this abrupt, stilted talk about organs and Godzillas. Yet, she seems like a lizard basking in the sun, and so—I'm left holding a scaly, unattached tail.

I rest my shoulder against the warm, smelly cedar (its scent is dry and enflamed) and give her my cocked eyebrow.

"Marjorie could make you a hot dog," I say.

I don't want to let Marjorie's daughter off the hook, but I don't want her to know how uninterested I am in her embarrassment, either. She's gazing up at me now, her head tilted, and I recognize that look from my own face—a sneer which the bright sunlight protects from reproach.

I squint fiercely back, though my own face is in shadow. She's shocked, and for a moment her face unfolds into a smooth sheet, and her mouth drops open as if to stretch the sheet even tighter. She closes her mouth and shades her eyes from the sun and also from my view. I can see the line of unsteadiness in her jaw.

"What?" she says irritably.

"Marjorie can make you a hot dog," I say flatly, a little louder than before. I'm happy for how absurd this inane phrase sounds when repeated.

She won't look at me, and certainly won't answer. She settles her head back on the shingles.

From where I stand, I could touch the top of her mossy head, and I don't think she would hit me because her position is vulnerable now. Still, yesterday's punch was anything but meek. She's no ordinary girl; she has spunk, the kind my mother used to have.

When my mother was old and roped up in veins like a blue calf, they would say she had spunk. Old, sperm-racked woman had a stockpile of spunk. That's why she lived longer than my father: she was waiting for her turn to have spunk. But when it came, it was useless, and her gloating eyes shone with fool's-gold fever. Everyone said, "My, hasn't she got spunk." and she smiled, and winked that dead wink. Her crumpled rag-paper eyelid blinked, "Yes, haven't I got spunk, and I'm not even flesh anymore, just a spit-wad of blue-ruled paper." Spunk—what a tasteless joke.

That's what I like about Marjorie's daughter: she's got old-woman spunk. She's not waiting until she's a hunk of dried flesh, she's getting her spunk right now. God only knows what she's going to do with it.

Marjorie walks past us into the kitchen. Her daughter and I

seem to make a point of not speaking as she passes. I, out of fear; she, out of sullenness. Marjorie comes back, carrying a flat pink pastry box which she takes to the picnic table, shouting urgently for people to move things out of the way. I steal a glance at her daughter once more, expecting her to look humiliated, at least for her behavior toward me. I keep forgetting; Marjorie's daughter is in her mid-twenties by now. You can't tell by her appearance—you'd have to saw her in half and count the rings.

"John," Marjorie calls, "John, come here. Guest of honor, everyone. Listen up. John's leaving us, as many of you know. Twenty-five years on the job."

General applause.

"That's what a head start'll get you, a pension before you're fifty. How about that? We'll miss you, John. All the best. Here's to the end of your career and the beginning of your golden years."

The white flagstone of cake is overgrown with blue roses. CONGRATULATIONS, it says.

"For he's a jolly good fellow," Marjorie chants.

Suddenly my head feels enormous. Everything seems so far away, and for a moment I'm relieved, but it's impossible to sustain an even blend of detachment and panic.

"For he's..."

"Jolly..."

"For..."

They come together somewhere in the middle and get on with it.

But now my head feels much too small, and I'm afraid that

16

if it keeps on shrinking, something will start to ooze out of the openings and I won't be able to hide it.

I don't know any of these people. I know Marjorie a little, because I drive her to work every day, but the rest of them are just beginning to wonder who I am. It's getting so bad that I.

Can't believe that I forgot this feeling. It's alright now; everything is fine. They're starting another round of song, and I've snapped clean over the threshold. I'll just stand here until it's over. There's no use trying to hold together: I'm barely visible anyway.

Now they're clapping and milling about, so I can head for the bathroom and wait until it's died down. I'm turning and bumping into people for a long time until I run smack into Marjorie's daughter and hear the mouth of a pint bottle clank against her teeth. She smiles and wipes a drip of whiskey off her dark, pretty chin. Marjorie looks over, crinkling her nose.

"Liann!" she snaps, frowning at the bottle.

"Oh Christ, Mom."

I'm stealing away, I think, but there's a sharp whistle and I turn around again.

"Here, catch."

I catch the pint bottle. Liann winks at me and walks back to her mother.

Of all the nerve. I go into the kitchen, put the bottle on the counter, think twice about it, then take a hit.

SUNDAY AFTERNOON

I HAVE a few short steps to the corner of Marjorie's street, and I take them leisurely. I don't know if anyone has seen me leave; they might, for instance, think I ran away.

My truck is down the block, pointed toward my house.

Yet it's a pointlessly long drive, not as if you were in the city; cities strut and pose, clack you under their heels as they grind out their cigarettes. You can furtively look up their skirts. But in the suburbs you move through an embarrassing conflagration of organs. The suburbs lie as level as a de-boned whore, as if someone had built a brothel with a ceiling clearance of two feet—all you can do is grope past a foot, round a thigh, up a finger. You can't ever get on top. Sometimes I think it would be better to live in the city, where at least you can see the whole body at once, even if you're forbidden to touch it.

My house is low, with hanging eaves and a wide, flimsy garage so aggressive that it plants its big, square mouth right on the edge of the sidewalk—its flat tongue of a driveway spreads out into the street, waiting to lick me in.

You'd think, after twenty-some years, that I would have discovered the great, gaping hole in the wall of my house that I know must exist. The builders must have left a corner unsealed, or the elements eroded some forgotten joint, because I never feel thoroughly indoors here. At night, when it's black outside, I fill each room with light to see if the house will hold it, or if the light is seeping out through some elusive puncture.

I turn the knob, which has never had much action, and the door falls open. But something in the way the latch clicks is feeble too soon—the door wasn't locked after all.

I hear a metallic growl, as if my house were clearing its copper throat in order to bellow an obscenity: the pipes are grumbling, someone is taking a shower. In the bedroom, strange clothing lies crumpled on the floor so gently I'm no longer afraid. I smell steam, and my shampoo. I know who it is: it has to be Stephan.

There is a faint smell of city in the room that I haven't encountered in more than a year. All the same.

"Stephan," I say, watching the water from the showerhead fail to affect his skin and curl away in a pique of steam. He doesn't hear me.

"Stephan, where exactly is your liver? I'm curious."

Stephan curls an arm out of the stall and flings a towel at my face so that I can't see him and can barely hear, then tries to crack me in the head but gets me with just the soft side of his wrist. I take off the towel and hold it out to him.

"Someone told me today she could feel the location of her organs. You don't even know where your organs are, do you, Stephan?"

Stephan has a body like a tractor trailer, a wood-chipper that destroys the evidence. It doesn't steer easily, and it doesn't go fast, but it's very, very healthy.

I'm referring to the way he eats. Stephan may be dangerous, but I don't think he's a mulcher. He looks reliable. I'm sure his guts are made of something that weathers well and feels good to the touch—silk, chrome, or papyrus. Stephan makes you want to slip your extremities into him, get your whole hand under his chest, as if you were dipping into a bin of silks so perfect your fingers feel wet and flush and.

He's probably never been sick a day in his life.

He's not sick now, because there are dirty dishes all over the place. Anyway, if Stephan were sick, he'd crawl under your house, not in it.

He puts his foot on the lid of the toilet, yanks the towel from my hand, and begins drying his shin.

"No particular organ," I say, "whatever you can come up with. Just point."

Stephan changes shins—he's being kind of rough with himself. Stephan's skin is the same color between his toes as it is between his shoulder blades. He doesn't let you focus on him very well or very much, so all you ever get is a general impression. It's even hard to tell which color he is (all over). He inspires faith in the curious to the same degree that he remains aloof: I believe you could take an axe to Stephan and fail to reveal anything new.

I've only seen him naked once: I was sitting in the dim bar of the club—as far into that place as I wanted to go—waiting for Stephan to finish work. The doors to the steam room burst open and a young boy wearing a fatigue jacket and carrying a briefcase shot through the bar and into the street. Stephan barreled after him, leaving a wake of steam—were it not for that lingering plume I would not have believed I'd seen his body at all. In a moment Stephan came back from the street with the briefcase. He streaked past me without a glance, swearing, into the innards of the club. Twenty minutes later he emerged, clothed and sleek, as if nothing had happened, and by then I wasn't sure if anything had.

"Are you conscious of no physical functions?" I ask.

Stephan points to the toilet.

"You're having an out-of-body experience," I say coldly, and leave him to his shins.

The distance he's traveled to get here is enough to make me anxious all by itself. You see, there's a wide, heavy bay nearby, with the longest bridge in the world. Not a suspension bridge, but a floating bridge, long enough to curve with the surface of the earth. I had thought myself safe from this sort of thing. I keep thinking: Stephan must have used some kind of naughty, occult conveyance.

It's late, though, and the last thing I want after the company picnic and all that obscene catsup waving, and the beautiful girl with the tangible guts and the antibiotic hair, is to be a flophouse for a dancing instructor, a panderer, and a sometime locker room attendant who has nothing to offer me in this part of the world.

But why is he here? Even if I asked, he wouldn't tell me. Is someone after him? (Is he after me?) If he thinks I skipped out on him, it's hard to imagine he'd wait a year to hunt me down. I've given him a lot of money, but I'm naive about such things. It might not have been enough. Still, that doesn't explain why he's here—unless the procurer has come to procure me for himself.

Curiosity is the first sign that you live in the suburbs. You can't afford to be curious when you're dealing with people from the city—at least the ones I know. It isn't because they're dangerous; it's just a courtesy. If you leave them alone and don't ask them what kind of ugly business they have with you, they might not ask what kind of ugly business you have with them.

Stephan is now looking very discreetly through my dresser drawers. I can tell that he's feeling sorry he didn't go pick on someone his own size. I don't want to watch him, or see him catalogue my clothes with his fingertips. This is the trick that I play on myself: if I can get out of this room before he finishes using my closet, then I can make it to my easy chair before he comes out; it's a version of hide-and-seek.

And here he is, wearing my robe. No, no one's left any clothes here, sir. My little man. We don't get many visitors in these parts, no sir, you can count on it. He looks uncomfortable, but that might be because the robe is too small. I'm hoping otherwise, because I have to get him out of my house.

I have at least ten books in my lap. I've been fondling them on the shelf, which is next to the chair, and pulling them down intermittently. Whenever I'm feeling restless, I like to limit my options arbitrarily: I can bounce my knees, but I

22

can't cross my legs without creating a natural disaster.

"Look," I say, "I don't know what you want, but—"

"Sorry I hit you."

"It didn't hurt," I respond without any feeling whatsoever. "I got hit yesterday, too." I'm sounding more familiar than I had intended.

"Don't tell me about it, okay?"

There it is, that funny accent he uses to make himself sound like a foreigner. That's part of what makes it so hard to be really forceful with Stephan; you always feel inclined to speak slowly and enunciate, so he'll understand what you're saying.

"It happened in a restaurant."

Stephan cocks his head and sits on the couch. I nod knowingly, but not because of anything I know.

"I was in the wrong place at the wrong time."

This is so plainly hilarious that Stephan scowls. "Well, I can see you haven't changed."

"Stephan?" I say.

He looks up, entirely inquisitive.

I make a face that shows him how trying his presence is. I can see that it's working.

"It isn't that I'm not delighted to see you."

He nods again, catches himself, then gets up and returns to the bedroom. I don't expect him to say anything else, and he doesn't.

He's dressed when he comes back out.

"Its just that I'm expecting people," I say, "and you know how that is."

He gives me an odd look, but then I knew he wouldn't believe me. He hesitates by the door, drops his eyes to my lap. I look down too, and see the pile of books vibrating on my bouncing knees, about to erupt. I hold still and grip the arms of my chair.

"Alright," he says. He slams the door on his way out, and is gone.

S U N D A Y   N I G H T

I sɪᴛ up gasping, but it isn't because of anything I've dreamed, since I haven't been able to sleep. My head pecks like a chicken, three times; then I roll back onto the mattress, and feel a nauseous wave go over me until I'm up again, wondering where I've just been. I remember looking at the ceiling—gray, with the consistency of regurgitated fluid. I feel that fluid in my stomach, and its continuity with the ceiling makes me feel as though I'm rising in the air. But my stomach isn't rising. It's resting heavy and still, as if the fluid were a mixture of water and plaster. Instead of thinking I'll throw up, I think the ceiling might belch down and drown me in paste. I'm looking straight ahead and level, and the ceiling isn't before me anymore: I'm not as nervous as I thought.

I wonder what's wrong with Liann, besides the Japanese horror movie she's got going inside her. That must be why she always looks so unconcerned—but as if she might bow down and swipe you with a branch. I can tell that she's worn-out and jittery. Being sick gives you stamina, I know: nothing lasts longer than weakness.

Which thrives on disruption. She's like a worm that can be severed in half and still live. You could argue that it isn't the same worm anymore, only something dissected into many lonely, floating parts.

Her skin isn't the continuous sheet of color that Stephan's is—in the yard I saw several hundred shades of pink under her fingernails alone—and it isn't a stained, mothy blanket like mine. My skin has been so wrinkled and darned and patched and snagged and burned with things that people have dropped on me when they have fallen asleep, that I haven't been able to bring myself to look at it in years.

I wonder what was wrong with Stephan.

I was asleep—wasn't I? It felt, for a moment, as if the front door were hit by a truck. But all my blood seems to have rushed to my tongue, and I can feel my toes curl under. Christ! There it goes hammering again, a sound to mutate the species.

I get up and walk through the house, into the living room, but I'm afraid to touch anything—as if I were already a ghost visiting and remembering a bygone pain. A swimming irritation is clouding my eyes, and I'd like nothing more than to interrupt this grayness with light. But the switches are all too far away, and the curious idea of light is now too remote, although if the house is coming down.

I see Stephan looking through my living room window. His arms are folded against the glass as he gazes into my living room. He keeps looking without blinking (his outer lids), but I know he's not staring: he's watching.

I yank the drapes together and open the door.

"Hello, Stephan."

He's already standing in front of the door with his hands in his pockets, but I'd swear that he hadn't had enough time to get there from outside the window.

"Hi," he says, stepping in as if he'd just been invited to dinner. His bad imitation of an accent serves him well: he never has to say the right thing.

"What kind of uniform is that?" Stephan asks.

"It's a sleeping uniform," I answer, checking the top button of my pajamas to make sure it's closed.

The pile of books is still in the easy chair, but I push them off so I can sit down. I don't want to create the possibility of Stephan sitting next to me on the couch. He watches me with a lively smile.

"Do you have a Coke in the refrigerator?"

I'm afraid that sending me to the kitchen is a ploy to get the easy chair for himself. I go anyway, but when I come back he's sitting at the far end of the couch with his feet up. I put down the can of Coke on the coffee table and take back the chair, angry at how possessive he's made me seem.

I've never been irritable with Stephan before. Irritating, maybe; I've tried to be abrasively nice, but I didn't have anything in mind when that started—it was just the only superior attitude I could sustain. I was very concerned, then, about impressing him; he always looked so impressed with himself.

"So what have you been up to?" Stephan asks, so off-handedly that it makes me wary. Normally it would have taken me a while to prepare an answer he'd accept. Now, however, the strangest thing I could do would be to talk about Liann; maybe that would make him leave.

"I met a girl today," I begin, and actually tell him a lot more about her than I know. In fact, I tell him some bald-faced lies, just to make the whole thing sound plausible. I'm careful not to say anything about trees and moss.

"You don't have any brains," Stephan says. He uses the wrong emphasis for what he means, and so it sounds as if he might just as easily have meant that I didn't have any calf's brains in the refrigerator. He also sounds as if he were half-shouting the sentence for the third time to a deaf person, even though he's only said it once, quietly. That's definitely a Stephan trick, that poor intonation. (Have I picked it up from him?) It takes practice. You have to silently recite the phrase over and over until it loses all sense. I've seen Stephan carry on conversations like this, as if he were reading an incoherent script in perfect English. It shakes people down to their bones.

At least I can't answer him, so I shrug, limiting the gesture to the tendons in my neck, then tell him about Liann's fingernails.

"She's very pretty," I say. "You'd like her."

"I wouldn't have expected it of you," Stephan says, "but if you say so."

"I haven't done anything."

"You really do have a double life, don't you?" Stephan asks. It's a dumb question, but he looks serious.

"No. I used to have a half-and-half life. Now I just have half of one, and by the end of the week I'll be free and clear of it all."

28

"What's happening at the end of the week?"

"I'm retiring."

Stephan bursts out laughing.

"What's the matter with that?"

Stephan has to finish laughing for a while. "I'm just not used to that kind of talk. People like you don't retire. The way you say it—what are you going to do, play golf?"

"No."

"Well?" he pursues. "What are you going to do?"

"I haven't thought about it, to tell you the truth."

"You're serious, aren't you?" he says, laughing more softly.

"Yes. And if that's all you want—I'm not retired yet, and I still have to be at work in the morning."

"Listen, if it's alright with you, I'd like to stay the night," Stephan asks without much inflection. "It's late, and I don't want to go back. I've been walking for—"

He's getting up.

I shrug. He's standing over me.

"There's an extra room at the end of the hall," I say. "Blankets and things in the hall closet."

Miraculously, he turns and walks away. I hear the door to the spare room open and close—and that puzzles me, because I know there's no bed in there, nothing but carpeting in fact.

It's done now, and it seems almost stupid, the whole thing, and I'm not going to bother thinking about any of it, because finally it's just too late.

MONDAY MORNING

I'VE driven to Marjorie's house to pick her up for work and stand idling in the driveway. The horn honking is over. She will look out now, between those two curtains, as always, to make sure it's me. Stephan is still in my house and knowing that makes me feel.

Marjorie's front door opens. Liann's in the shadow behind her, hugging her goodbye. Yesterday everyone seemed to have a professional air of strangeness, but today they're just perplexing. I'm pretending to look for something on the floor of the truck, and feel like an idiot because I remember that all the stuff I told Stephan last night isn't true. Now Marjorie's inside the car, but I keep feeling around under the seat until I hear the door slam.

"You say that every year," I say to Marjorie, unsure I heard her correctly.

"And every year I think I mean it," she says. "Next time somebody else can do the company picnic. I'm pooped out."

We ride in silence. A cloud has spread across the road and the trees have settled into stillness clear as a pool. Unwelcome thoughts expand to fill this solemn gap, and I gasp suddenly, then catch my breath: I momentarily forgot that I am not alone.

Marjorie mistakes this for hangover grief. "You're pooped out, too," she says.

I don't answer because I'm thinking about Liann. She also has to be at the plant by eight. She must have her own car. Several years ago, she worked at the plant for a summer and rode with us every day. I know this for a fact, although I can't remember her well.

"Is your daughter back with you?" I ask, wishing I hadn't.

Marjorie sighs ruefully. "And how. I thought that if I got her a job she might clear out of my house. I guess she had some sort of falling-out with the construction outfit where she worked before—but she won't give me a straight answer."

"Would you like to start riding with her?" I say.

Marjorie gives a derisive laugh. "Not if I want to get to work before noon," she says with a snort of bitter fondness.

I park as close as I can to the plant door because Marjorie walks so slowly. There's no hurry, but walking across the parking lot isn't particularly enjoyable and I don't see any reason for dragging it out. Marjorie's not much older than me, but I feel my age in dog years when I'm shuffling along beside her. This car-pool thing was my idea, insurance that I would get to work every day. But I've been doing it for over twenty-four years: you'd think I could manage on my own by now.

She's gone as soon as we clear the entrance; I walk up the half flight of stairs and down the hall to my office while she strolls off to God knows where on the factory floor.

There's a stack of flimsy request forms in my in-box. I detest such forms, because I have to type out a purchase order for each one. Every little doodad these jokers think should get stuffed inside a mattress has to be ordered separately. My typewriter is on. Someone's been in here already.

The old IBM is spattered with correction fluid, and the indentations on the keys are filled with dust that has been lacquered over by fingertips. I have to type carefully, because the seven-layer purchase-order forms are very expensive and I'm accountable for them; if I make a mistake I can't throw them away, which is why I have seven colors of correction fluid on top of my desk. This order is addressed to the printer for law labels:

1000 @ $00.10 ea.
as per previous order #S 10034

That's right, I think, but it's impossible to proofread invoices and purchase orders, because you can't misspell a number. I have to compare each figure on the request form with the corresponding figure on the purchase-order form and see if they match.

It's the seven layers that do me in. I get nervous, as if I were plodding through a hall of mirrors where every gesture is repeated again and again. The errors shift and multiply even as you turn to search for them: soon every stroke looks like a mistake.

My arms ache, and it never ends. I have to tear the layers apart and do all kinds of esoteric things with them. The green goes to the supervisor, the pink into the alphabetical Supplier file, and the yellow goes into limbo until it gets stapled to the supplier's invoice, which is sent to Accounts Payable. The blue goes into the notebook for profit and expenditure estimates in the bottom desk drawer. The goldenrod is filed by date in Orders Receivable. The white, the original, is mailed. I can't think what to call the off-white one—a spare, I guess. I type and stuff the envelopes, then give them to the receptionist, who checks to make sure the right orders are in the right envelopes. There is no secretary.

When I'm done, I don't feel bad at all. I like the way the carbons smell, and the whispery crinkling of the pages. For a little while, I can close the door, and people will think.

The *Handbook of Occupational Titles* is open on my desk. I'm using one hand to keep the pages spread and the other on myself, under the desk. I spit in my hand and rub one finger up the hard stem and around the lip of the head, bringing a feeling similar to the resonant, eerie sound of a finger rimming a water glass. This part of the book is about Liann:

Entry number 780.685-014 STUFFING MACHINE OPERATOR—

tends machine that cleans and fluffs filling and blows it into prefabricated covers to form mattress or other upholstered pads...

weighs filling material such as cotton or sisal to obtain specified weight and dumps into hopper...

33

of machine. Places cover over discharge tube...

and starts machine that cleans and fluffs and blows filling material into cover...

removes filled cover and closes end.

Under the desk I close a fistful of pilfered sisal, rasp it upwards, then throw it away.

Places pad on table and strikes it with a wooden pole to...

I miss the puffing of machinery outside the office, and I have to open the door so that the sound can return in physical waves. I sit down again and lean my elbows on the desk, cradling my face in my hands above the book, and smell the sisal on my palm. I listen for the sound of the stuffing machine, which I can't really distinguish, and start to dream again: *Dumps into hopper. Places cover over discharge tube and...*

MONDAY AFTERNOON

I FEEL as if I've had an unpleasant encounter with these trees before, and maybe I did, early this morning, when I drove past them in the other direction. But then, I have a hard time telling the difference between good and bad things once they've been committed to memory.

I'm driving Marjorie home, and she's dropping hints that I should stop off at her house and help her purge her yard of picnic debris. The trees are making me flinch as we pass under them, and I try to conceal the small jolts they're creating in my neck. But it's not the trees; it's whatever I was thinking when we drove past them on the way to the plant. I'm afraid that if I glance in the rearview mirror, I might catch a glimpse of their morning side, and remember.

Marjorie's yard is hiding its debris very well, and I'm personally inclined to ignore it. I want to go home, to make sure Stephan is gone. And I don't want to run into Liann, not after all the ridiculous things I said about her last night—to Stephan. I never should have mixed the two of them up in my head like that.

I tell Marjorie I have some errands to run before five, and go home.

The house looks empty from the outside. The door from the garage to the kitchen is locked. I can tell there isn't anyone here. Just more dirty dishes, and wet towels on the bathroom floor. I wonder if Stephan is amphibious.

The towels I can stand, but the dishes I've got to clean up right away, as soon as I change my clothes.

My house is haunted with slowly moving icebergs of afternoon light. I am frozen inside, in front of the kitchen window. My hands are numb in the dishwater tub and the damp cuffs of my sweater are like itchy scabs reluctant to slough themselves off. Linoleum, tile, and stainless steel are so lucid and hard, I feel a distant guilt associated with them. I'm suspicious of anything solid. My hands and feet must be chalky and bloodless by now—single loaves of stale bread, airy and white in the center. Stephan isn't here. But for some reason, that isn't good enough.

There's something I'm forgetting. This fear feels too much like a minor flu, which means that my willful body has swallowed the germ. I wish I could remember what it was. It's no use standing here, feeling my solar plexus fire warning flares along my nerves.

Back in the truck, I feel like a bat stretched out in front of a sunlamp. My little bat heart is heating up, and already my wings are cauterized so that the light no longer shines through them. My overextended elbow joints—where the folds fan out like flattened umbrellas—are going to pop their sockets soon, and I think they will ache forever. I ought to be home, hanging from the ceiling like a good vampire bat, but I'm out in it now, and the heat is like a stake in my heart, painful and relieving.

I'm coming up on the floating bridge, which I'll take at ninety. The bridge curves ever so slightly to the right, so fractional that I can't feel myself adjusting the wheel; I simply have to trust my will to live as I follow the stretch of faith that lies so unavoidably between here and there.

Stephan walks in the emergency lane.

I saw the figure a moment ago, shirttails flying, but I didn't believe in it.

Stephan, hands in his pockets, has a long way to go, and has been walking for a long time, no doubt.

I didn't stop, and now there are miles between us, which means that I'm still going to the city, but no longer to find Stephan—at least not yet. Finally I come to the other side of the bridge.

I park the truck in the weeds of a vacant lot.

I used to come to this place, this narrow edge of the city called the Rattail, almost every day, and I was never happier, but I could have died. I never took an apartment, because I never wanted to stay that long. I would park in this same place and begin to look for Stephan immediately, starting with the place where he worked and lived. I've never seen Stephan's room, because it's way in the back of the building; at my insistence, our business was always conducted in the bar.

The antique, barely visible sign could be painted onto the brickwork with mustard: a mustachioed strong-man in a striped tank suit is standing next to the words "Physical Culture."

The other sign, the one over the door, is just as bad, but it's not so old. It's a picture of an arm making a fist. The fist isn't going to hit anyone; it might be flexing, but it's slung sort of low, and the part of the shoulder that's included in the picture is stooping. The gesture is violent but intent, the kind of gesture that creates its own private communication.

The accordion grate is open, and there's a guy sitting in the stairwell reading a magazine. They had to get someone to watch the door when the place got too popular, but I remember once, before they did, Stephan and I were walking out of the bar and there was an old guy asleep in the doorway. Stephan leaned on my shoulder confidentially.

"Want to hear a fairy tale?" he said.

With Stephan, this meant neighborhood gossip.

"That old man? His prick is gray, and when he gets excited, he waves it around and throws his voice, and you can hear the thing trumpet like a trained elephant, can you believe it?"

I walk past the doorway and stand at the corner. There's a person across the street whom I don't know but looks very familiar. It seems strange to have come all this way, to park the truck and walk a block just to stand on the corner across from this person. I think I'll wait the light through and stare blankly at the signal, just to disconcert him. It's a trick that I learned from Stephan, and I'm glad that I did, because it reminds me that he's not around.

The man is crossing the street and I'm directly in his path. His shoulder slams into mine, and instead of yielding, I shove him back. He turns, and I meet his earnest, hesitant eyes. I can tell he mistakes my indifference for longing. It's all very specific, and at the same time pointedly vague.

"What did you mean by that?" he asks, spouts.

I give him the same blank look, and he turns away, deliberately shrugging and shaking his head. I know his glands have let loose a syrup of anger and shame and that, for the moment, he's all alone, moving through his own density. I watch him veer into the doorway of Physical Culture.

I begin walking down the block. I nod and smile at the parking meters, just for fun. The sky is split down the middle between a black, ponderous cloud and a blue-yellow sun. It's enough to make you burst out laughing. Tires snicker on the pavement, the manhole covers chuckle sharply, and a siren shrieks like a girl who's been barreled over by a runaway ice cream truck. I picture the parking meters nodding back, each one bending cutely as I pass it. But I'm not even nodding to them anymore. I'm walking very conservatively now because I want nothing to interrupt this.

I don't know what I was afraid of here. It was silly to stop coming to the city. I can remember walking down the street feeling the quality of the day, stepping smoothly without pausing, so that the movement of my feet would be soothing, and the city would seem enormous and light and unperturbed. My head could be crashing and narrow with pain, but I'd feel anchored enough to let my mind float above it without fear.

The river has opened in front of me, curled its smart little finger and poked me in the ribs. The street dead-ends on the shore, next to a restaurant where I can hear a whole flat of glasses shivering against each other in the kitchen. The retaining wall by the water is pressing into my stomach, and I lean out, waist-high, as if I wanted to be sick. But I feel good today, and I don't need to look for internal evidence. I smell the water instead. It stinks, and I can feel the pleasant sensation of organs responding up to my inner ear.

I watch the warm sunlight struggle on the surface of the water then slip under, like a diving bird caught by an unexpected forest of kelp, and another thought occurs to me: Stephan might have reached the city by now.

I turn my back on the river because the light is too bright and it's distracting me from the delicate heat. I can feel it on the sleeve of my calfskin jacket, and I want to feel it on the back of my head. The restaurant is one I know, and I'm pretty sure, rather sadly, that it's where I'll end up waiting. I'll go have some coffee. I feel indescribably good, which is making me nervous, since it's gone on about as long as I can stand.

The walls are a deep teal green and the furniture is all dark wood. The place is beautiful entirely by accident, although it's beginning to comprehend itself a little more each time I come here. Yet, whenever they take off the vinyl tablecloths, it seems bare and noisy and suddenly unconscious again. It used to be dopey and sullen, but now it's almost dead around the edges, as if it had been sent into a catatonic state by some bad experience.

I'm rubbing my eyes after handling the dirty salt shaker. I

can see blue and yellow ribbons on my lids, now fading, and the coffee is so hot that I'm sure it's irradiating me, but more important, it's promising me a long visit. A new row of paintings is for sale on the back wall, and I don't want to look at them. Out the window, the light is so white it hurts. I wonder how I could have gotten so upset, why I had to rush here like this, as if I'd die anywhere else. I try to keep wondering, because other, worse thoughts are threatening to return and.

Inundate me. If they keep whipping around and blending together so fast, I won't be able to breathe. Fast and slow, faster, as I breathe, so that nothing gets out of hand. Sip the coffee.

It's hot enough to scald the nerves, which are moaning, wailing and waving their outraged tendrils so that everything is clear for a second, then blackened with mourning, laid low to the ground and limp.

Let me talk to you now: I don't know who you are, but that isn't the issue, I'll make you listen. Put your fingers on your forehead and feel your skull. Pull your fingers down and feel your eyebrows slide against the bone. It's disgusting, isn't it? If you didn't do it, it's because you already knew what it would feel like. Let me tell you about the time I pierced my eyelids. No? Then just imagine it. Your temples sweat, and you think you might die, then you're blinded by blood and you fall into weak, hopeless fear. Not the fear that you won't get to the other side, but fear without those hopeful conditions. It's a pure feeling, and I wish you could witness it.

The first person Stephan ever introduced me to was a man six-foot five, with an orange beard that I remember distinctly because the hairs were twice as thick as any human hair I had ever seen. They were curly, too—tight, wild curls. He took off my shirt and wrapped my upper body in barbed wire, under my armpits and down my arms, then dressed me in a padded vest, a starched white dress shirt, an evening jacket, and took me out dancing.

In the cab he said nothing; he was plainly interested in only the necessary facts, not in the fantastic embellishments—a very practical person, someone who didn't have to make believe about something he was really doing. We didn't take a table or order drinks but went straight to the dance floor, where he crushed me to his chest, spun me around, and turned me with precision. He only gave in once: his tongue shot out and licked a drop of sweat from my temple. I could feel the trickles of blood run down my waist and between my legs; now and then, when I bowed my head, I could see little dimes, quarters, and pennies of blood fall to the floor, as if through a hole in my pocket, and get scuffed into streaks by a herd of feet.

In his room, he unwound the length of barbed wire, then rubbed a mixture of mustard and gunpowder into each of the wounds, one puncture at a time, starting on the left and moving right. My body is still covered with tiny black buttons. I know where they are, I can feel them through my shirt.

When he finished, everything else was just as hasty, in his bathroom with the glaring light. I folded my arms on the edge of the sink and lowered my head against them. Then I blacked out—from the waist up, I think, because his hands, which were fleshy and warm and ordinary on my thighs, were numb on the back of my neck. Standing up, with my head at that strange level in space, I grew curious about the way sensations traveled *down,* and how my legs were then privileged with feeling.

I'd love to have a zipper in my abdomen, to open and close my guts when the body's solitude became too much. I'd love to live in there, bleeding profusely, in the threads of molecules, and feel nothing but cell against cell, burnishing each other into reproductivity.

I want to hold my entrails to my cheek. I want to kiss them and say how much I love them. I want to soak in my lonely, atomic brain and sob through a hole in my head. I want to live as a warm pool of blood—a close, warm, unafraid darkness of blood.

MONDAY NIGHT

A PALE, fleshy girl is lumped on a single bed: a paperweight holding down the parchment bedsheets, lying limp in the humidity. The sheets are trilled and skittered into curves—still and cottony and damp—bleached white and woven by sadness. Her pale skin suggests an interior pallor, no darkness inside, no invisible black rhythm. If she ever rises, the imprint of her body will be a gray shadow of sweat and city soot. I can just make out a vibration of breathing, and I'm shocked that she's alive after all.

But I'm seeing her through a doorway. A man named Terry has told me that he doesn't know where Stephan is staying these days. Terry doesn't remember me. We all went out drinking once, and we ended up here, at Terry's place. It was only a social call.

Stephan really does give dancing lessons, but he's found that the kind of people who come to a young man named Stephan for dancing instruction often benefit more from being introduced to each other (or to me) than from learning

how to dance—and they're very understanding when he mul-
tiplies his rates.

I met Stephan in the bar that occupies the front room of
Physical Culture—he was working there, checking towels,
and slept in a room on one of the upper floors. He explained
about this dancing thing, using a lot of words, for him.

"Anyone can do it," he said. "I took a few lessons, and then
put an ad in the paper."

"Don't you ever get a student who knows more than you
do?" I asked, hoping he wasn't a wincing, tender idiot whom
I'd have to talk out of some hopeless scheme.

"Yes, but they're too embarrassed to admit it because
they've usually come for other things."

I was surprised at how congenial he was, and wanted to
end the conversation before it died. I suspected that Stephan
didn't have more than two or three exchanges in him before
he grew irrevocably bored.

"It's getting late," I said, and stood.

"You're not going inside," he observed, keenly.

I made a face, and he must have assumed some meaning
on my part.

"Why do you think I'm giving dancing lessons?" he said in a
confidential tone.

I wasn't sure what he meant. "No—" I said, then gave him
my best ironic smile. "I'm shy."

He shrugged. "Anyway. Come dancing sometime."

And that's how it started with Stephan.

It's getting late. I've said goodbye to Terry and I can't think
of anywhere else to go.

A blinking fluorescent tube hangs crookedly from the hallway ceiling, pulsing over me like a ray gun. I'm sitting on the stairs, not because I need a rest, but to distance my skull from the throbbing light.

There used to be a human brain not too far from here, in Theo's apartment. He had bought it somewhere (yes, it's possible), and put me on the floor, on all fours, while it burned on the grate in the fireplace. It burned ferociously, and I wonder—now, for the first time—what preparations he had made to make it flame. I can see him basting it with Everclear in a crystal bowl.

He held my head, thumbs fitting into the dishes of my temples, training my eyes on the fire. But what I remember is: the coarse blue rug, its bite on my knees and the balls of my fists.

I allowed the rug fibers to heal into my skinned knees. If I pulled up the legs of my trousers right now, I could examine a pair of bluish scars. It's time to leave. The fluorescent tube is pointing its pulse at Terry's door; I'd be terrified to live in that room.

Someone else lives near here: Faye. She knows Stephan as well as anyone, in fact she took dancing lessons from him. I'm guessing that Stephan's students know him best, since they've seen him in a particular role of servitude, and no matter how majestic and terrible he makes himself out to be, they can always turn around and pay him. In my conjuring, I can imagine only one epiphany for Stephan: he teaches a helpless and penniless imbecile to dance; he imposes the esoteric precision of a rumba on a man or woman too poor to afford the slimmest desire, someone whose impoverished

46

mind accepts his advice without joy or design or gratitude or obligation. It's funny that Stephan's epiphany, to me, equals his denigration and uselessness. But he's too arrogant and acquisitive to reach anything lofty; the most graceful arc that his future could follow would be downward.

I was in Faye's apartment when Stephan showed her how to waltz. She was a tough customer, because she didn't know what she wanted. I think Stephan brought me along for a second opinion. I couldn't help him, at least in any practical sense. I sat on her rose-colored sofa draped with crochet antimacassars that her grandmother made, drinking her off-brand bourbon, and watched them dance side by side, their empty arms stretched out in front of them—not imploring, but arms that encircled and embraced the vacancy. Faye is a girl who wants to be a boy who wants to be a transvestite: "frozen TV dinners," in Stephan's vocabulary. Their feet moved precisely, carefully manipulating the air; their faces frowned in concentration, as if they were afraid of stepping on the toes of their own rapture. Faye wanted to know how to lead, so the two of them never danced together, always side by side. It was a legitimate dancing lesson, alright. I went with him again, a couple of times. Other than Terry, I think Faye is the only person who has ever seen Stephan and me together outside of Physical Culture.

I seem to be walking toward her building, although the idea of seeing her face seems beyond the reach of either memory or anticipation. I can see her clearly now—as I press the button in the lobby that corresponds to her apartment, the one with the scratched-off masking tape above it, the ragged contours spelling F-A-Y-E in a deteriorating alphabet. The black Bakelite button is gouged and scratched too, as if most of Faye's callers had claws.

She's home. The glass door gives a highly charged death rattle, and I push it open urgently, but with a twinge of revulsion, as if I were performing a tracheotomy. Faye is leaning on the buzzer, because the rattle follows me into the elevator, which is coated inside with that blue-flecked enamel you can find in my self-cleaning oven. I could easily feel like a dressed bird in here without giving it a second thought.

It's the door at the end of the hall, where the fire exit should have been. The fire exit is in Faye's apartment. Faye's room is nothing but a has-been walk-in closet spliced to a former hallway. There's still a red light above her window that leads to the fire escape. Faye is very vain, I think, because the original bulb must have burned out years ago, which means that she keeps replacing it.

The door is cracked open for whoever pushed the buzzer downstairs.

"Faye?"

"John!"

Her red fingernails are arrayed along my wrist before I can look at her face. The red light and the rose couch are nearer to each other than I remembered.

"John, what happened to you?"

My skin is tingling, searching itself for an incriminating mark.

"I mean, where have you been?"

"Oh—just—" I'm relieved, briefly, that nothing shows, even

before I shrug. Faye moves a heap of clothing off the sofa.

"Sit on the divan, John."

Faye issues statements like an anxious, crooked physician filling out a prescription for morphine. She even looks the other way while I lower myself.

She's lit on a straight-backed chair. I sense that I'm about to say something, but she's reached for a cigarette, and I close my lips.

"Cigarette?"

I shake my head, then, "I haven't been smoking."

Faye shakes her head, too. "You have great self-control. I don't have any."

I laugh. "That's a luxury."

Faye could be kissing the little flame goodnight, the way she blows on the match. "Luxuries," she says, "are supposed to be expensive. Doesn't that leave me out?"

"Necessities are expensive," I say quickly, trying to be clever. "It's the luxuries that are free."

Now I'm sure that she's happy to see me, because her eyes are glittering. "If they're free, then why can't I afford them?"

"Because you have to have all the necessities first."

Faye exposes her throat and laughs. My mind is racing to profound things, which are always too close to absurdity to utter. I'm not sure whether this notion is pathetic or grand, but maybe it's both, and that's the tragedy of it: pathetic grandeur. I feel ridiculous, festering such thoughts in the presence of this girl. She looks sly, smiling to one side—and in full drag, she's putting on the airs of a woman by trying to imagine that she doesn't know how.

Stephan bought her a dress one night, a flowered, fifties summer thing with a constructed waist, flared skirt, and padded bosom. The two of us were rounding the corner to her building when Stephan stopped, told me to wait, and ran back the way we had come. I thought he had probably gone off to get cigarettes, but when he returned with the dress in his hand, I recalled having glimpsed it earlier, among the wares of a street peddler two blocks back. I remember that moment, because it struck me that Stephan must have been thinking about the dress the whole time we'd been walking in silence. If he had decided against it, I would have never known that ruminant aspect of his mind. I took the knowledge as a cautionary gift.

Skinny girl, with short hair, no makeup, and enormous bare feet—when Faye put on that dress, she looked like a thirteen-year-old boy. We were all astonished.

It's why I never underestimate Stephan.

Faye is biting a long fingernail: she pulls it away, then glares at it, and giggles. "I forgot," she says. "They're fake."

She stares at her nails as if she were recovering a recent idea. "John, I've been thinking tonight, now listen."

She's been rehearsing something in the mirror, and I'm about to become a miracle existing in her head. She's trembling a little, and I wish she would change the forthcoming subject, because I know what will happen next: she's going to disclose some bloated detail of her imagination because I arrived here in the midst of it. She's too tipsy to remember that once imaginary things are spoken, they're about as useful as a puddle of leaked blood.

"It seems as if I'm always getting ready," she says seriously. "First I'm getting dressed, then I'm getting drunk, then all of a sudden I'm just recovering so I can start all over again."

I remember my brittle arrival in the city today, the bright light and the scarecrow people and the sound of shivering glass. It's like a sentimental hangover I'm experiencing in advance. I've realized that I'm not about to ask Faye if she's seen Stephan, because I'm no longer looking for him. I'm grateful for Faye's nocturnal vehemence.

"There just isn't anything for me to do!" she concludes.

"I have nothing to do either," I say automatically, and I know that my face reveals my condition, the exact time of day, the extent of my injuries, and several weaknesses I'd forgotten I had.

Faye is filling two glasses, and I think I can tell from the level of the liquor she's pouring how sorry she is for speaking openly with me.

"Oh, come on," she says with a sour inflection. "I know thousands of things you can do. More than you're aware of, I'm sure."

"I doubt it."

Faye's tears are prevented from falling because her eyes have widened to accommodate them. I hope I don't have to maintain her surprise all night in order to keep them there.

"Where did you come from?"

She doesn't expect me to answer. She is full of her own grief—and when you are grieving, everyone who comes to your door is confused and speechless, and tries to bear an

51

offering. You have special dispensation in your grief: the visitor can aid you, or mutter something reverential, or abuse you in a way that only demonstrates your virtue—and so you faint away from the door when you let them in.

"I'm sorry," Faye says, "I didn't mean to make you uncomfortable."

I can't even remember what she said, and she knows it.

"You're off in another world, aren't you?" She slaps my cheek gently, but I can feel her fingers trembling. "Never mind, let's dance."

This is something new. She has my wrists. Faye's never shown any interest in me before, and I've never concluded what her interests might be—I've always had the impression that she doesn't know either. This is the first time I've seen her without Stephan. Faye leads well. I don't know what dance we're doing, but I don't need to, because everything I do seems to be entirely up to her. I'm impressed—with Stephan, to think that he's actually taught her to do this—and I wonder if she knows how feminine she is, smiling out from behind a coil of loose hair. She's taller than I am, but it still feels as though she were looking up at me—yes, she's elaborately feminine. She's tipping her head back, and closing her eyes: she's vanishing away, but holding me firmly. Her hands make me feel tiny, fitting preciously into the small of my back. I feel like a pony, driven by the gentle laying on of hands. She's unaware of me watching her, and I am barely intuitive enough to follow the next step. But Faye is an intelligent woman, and I trust her.

She lifts her head up straight and opens her eyes. Her

52

arms fall away in futility, and I see that her efforts were, if anything, more successful for me than for her. That was the point of coming here, I realize, but the agenda has changed between then and now, so that being distracted is nothing but my own personal lapse. I should not have let her slip away.

"I'm so stupid!" she says, stiffening her arms and clenching her fists. "I'm so stupid. I don't know what I'm trying to prove. I hate this."

"Faye, you aren't stupid," I say, but I'm annoyed that she's brought things invariably back to her own grief. This is predictable, in people like her, yet I can't help wanting a little sympathy for myself. "You could always go to Scandinavia, you know—get yourself decked out with a dick and everything," I say jokingly, but not without impatience.

"Just stop it right there, John," she says.

"Would you like to know how they do it?"

She glares at me angrily.

I beckon her with my finger, and she responds, minimally, by turning her body toward me and crossing her arms.

"They cut off a strip of flesh here," I touch the slight roll above her hip bone with a finger. "Then they wrap it up and graft it on there." I take her hand, turn it palm up, and point to the veins on her wrist. "Then they leave it for a while to grow into the blood supply."

A rueful giggle emerges from Faye's lips. "Talk about a fist-fucker, eh?" she says cavalierly.

I smile, with relief.

Faye jerks her wrist away. "You go to hell!"

She drops her arms to her sides. "I'm sorry, John I don't

know what's the matter with me." The hands at her sides are clenching. "I was doing fine until you showed up."

I can see a milky poison sliding over her eyes, signaling another sudden ejaculation of anger.

"I'm sorry, too," I say, but not genuinely enough. She's stung my cheek with a flat palm, uncurled at the last moment.

Faye yelps in surprise, then a sticky sob catches in her throat, and the effort of bringing it out returns her to the cusp of rage. Her hand lands purposefully on my ear. She has snapped it back now, as if from a dangerous animal, and holds her stinging fingers bundled in the other fist, raising them to her lips. A fake nail has torn loose and dangles from the cuticle.

I can sense the degeneracy of terror affecting her, and I reach for her pair of hands. They need to be held still, so the panic can subside. But as I place my liver-spotted hands over hers, very close to her lips, the rage returns with a virility she seems to welcome. I understand that it's nothing personal as she flails her hands at my head, and pulls.

My head hits the wall, and I can feel the impact of her fists about my face and shoulders, but not the pain. My arms are up, defending, and trying to steer her to the lower regions of my body, where the damage will be private. I cannot have my face destroyed. I'm unused to this well of ferocity. Faye and I are not gaming with each other; she doesn't know what she's doing, and I need to stop her. My arms reach out to find her, but flee back to protect my head again. I taste blood on my thick, salty lips—the size of my lips is now worthy of awe. They are swelling and bursting leaks. I'm on the floor, and

Faye is kicking me, heaving me up from the ground by my hair and dropping me. I summon all my will to hold my body together, and stop her, but my lips are too puffy to move, so I have no clue what I've been screaming—the cracks and squishes inside me are loud enough to prevent me from hearing my voice. Fear is noisy, very very noisy.

Everything is still. Faye's cheek is pressed against the window glass. She's exhausted. I decide I'm going to let her watch me climb onto the sofa. My arms and legs can hardly support me for their electric vibrations, but I am curiously remote about them. I lower my head to the arm of the couch. The starched white lace of the antimacassar feels like a mass of cables and harsh jute ropes, so I snatch it out from under my bruised cheek.

Faye arrives quickly and takes the bit of lace from my hand. She looks at me sorrowfully but quietly, for she is still a long way off. She's surprised—she thinks I have moved her lace to keep from spilling blood on it. She would like to say she's sorry now but has decided she won't. I can see that she's never done this before. And I know that it's the kind of thing she'll do again and again, although whoever she does it to next won't be scared, because it'll be official.

I'm taking her hand in mine. It's relaxed, but I think she would rather have it to herself. If she wants to be a man, this is the part she has to learn: yes sir, little girl, you have to hold my hand afterward. Yes, I will love you for it. You are alone, all alone. There's nothing you can do to make me hate you, and that will show you just how well you know me. Take it like a man, Faye.

TUESDAY MORNING

I AM looking at a square of canned ravioli that was transformed into a bad thing when I wasn't watching. It failed to reach the garbage pail and is welded to the linoleum, where it looks like a lesion on the body of my house. I don't enjoy finding relics of Stephan here—I can feel the aftermath of his sudden appearance on my face; my eye looks like a ravioli, too, though not as stale as the one I am about to pick up. The sun is beating on it. I can sympathize.

Light is flooding the kitchen, and I am here looking at the bloody ravioli, instead of being in my office. I should call and tell them I have a third-degree ravioli on the floor and that it's spread to my face, or I should call and say that I am sick—a welterweight virus has attacked me in my sleep. I should call Marjorie. She hasn't been picked up for work, and has probably gone into limbo by now.

But first I have to create a cause for the face I saw in my rearview mirror, and from what I remember, I'd have to throw myself into a mattress stuffer to accomplish that. My imagination isn't up to the scenarios necessary to explain my bruises as an ordinary consequence. I wish Faye were still hovering over me with her rags full of ice. I should go back there. Like it or not, a beating is the basis for a relationship —a conspiracy you can enter into. I'm not being weak, because if I were, I'd still be feeling queasy on Faye's rose-colored couch, instead of eyeing my wall phone. Still, I have the salty brain of an accident victim, replaying the scene over and over in my mind as if, by the sheer repetition, it could come to seem less accidental. I wish I could wrap Faye around a telephone pole for evidence.

There is only one thing for me to do—I go through the kitchen door to the garage. An axe stands by the pile of cordwood I bought for the fireplace. My left arm wails at any contact with the axe handle, but I can drag it around. Behind the truck, in the small space between the bumper and the door, I raise the axe for a downward swing—it's the only way it can gain enough velocity to do damage—it falls, blunt side down, and splinters a corner of the taillight. I will have to gnaw away at the truck like a metal mouse.

(The phone is ringing.) My sick arm rises on call, and I let the butt of the axe swoop sideways. The red plastic brake light shatters. As the muscles in my arm shriek, the axe cracks on the bumper, bending it down from its bolts. Before the truck can arrange an expression of despair, I swing the axe five times, into the same confluence of metal objects, until tears invoked by my involuntary posture sting my eyes.

In the cab of the truck, I fish a rag from under the seat and wrap it around the axe head. Smash. At the window above the steering wheel: a spider's web. I catch my eye in the rearview mirror—I'm an image of the axe's impact. I put my face right up to the glass, trying to match the peak of my injuries to the epicenter of the break.

When I climb down, I can feel my legs, and I'm disgusted by the ignorant stability they have provided throughout this crime. I fold them up, to punish them for their subversive integrity, and sit on the oily pavement, which is suddenly cool.

My battered head rests against my battered bumper, and I press my lips to a pink powdered edge of shattered plastic. The phone is ringing again, and I pull myself up and through the side door.

The phone on the kitchen wall is throwing a tantrum—I wonder how I ever found enough sympathy for that wail, enough to pick up the thing and cradle it in the crook of my neck.

If it rings twice more, I'll answer.

"Hello."

"John!" It's Marjorie.

"I had an accident with the truck."

"Are you alright?" Her voice is lusty with alarm.

"Yes," I say. "A few bruises. Are you at the plant?"

"Liann drove me over."

"Could you please let them know what's happened, that I won't be in today?"

"Of course I will," Marjorie says.

"I'll be there tomorrow to pick you up," I interject hastily.

I've embarrassed her. She blusters around for a moment, then I say goodbye weakly, press the switchhook, and feel surrounded by silence—I let the receiver go, afraid it will ring. The receiver hits the wall, bobs on its springy cord, and settles into a muffled drone. My hands are hot from the phone—no, it's a thought, but one that's started in my hands instead of my brain. It can't be a very good thought, I realize, if it's so wary of being recognized. Oddly enough, my brain is too squeamish for these things—as if wringing my hands could shake them out. If only I could peel back my fingernail and pull out the thought with a pair of tweezers.

Stephan doesn't know my phone number. I don't know how he got my address. I wonder where he is? That's how unreliable I am. I should have known something would happen to me if I went into the city, and now it's followed me here. I think Stephan came to my house to plant a curse on me. I'm a sacrificial chicken, and the first thing I did was fly straight into the city to have my neck wrung. I should have known the minute I saw the scratchings on Faye's doorbell.

I can't think about curses, because whatever he had in mind for me was probably much worse. Stephan isn't the kind of person who explains himself. All he has to do is pass through without a word to wreck your life. My sleeve has crept up my arm, and the flesh is exposed, something I don't even want to see myself. Once, when the button sprang off my cuff at work, I had to go home sick.

It's time to get dressed now, if nothing else. I'll stand under the shower, then put on clean clothes, which will hurt where they cling to the bruised skin.

My bathroom is spotless and empty. I get a towel out of the linen closet and my clothes—a new cotton shirt and my favorite black trousers—out of the dresser drawer. I drop them on the carpet outside the bathroom and turn on the shower, then wait in the bedroom for the room to fill up with steam. When it's ready, I quickly shed my dirty things and go in, past a misty white mirror that is too preoccupied to show me a shadow, and step into the shower, closing the sliding door. There's nothing in here but me, a bottle of dish soap, and a razor. Without stopping, I lather my body, face, and hair, and shave with my eyes closed against the sting of detergent, my head tipped back to avoid the shower's hard jets. I step forward and rinse, guiding sheets of water with my hands, barely brushing the skin.

I dry carefully, then reach for my clothes. The stiff, new shirt conforms reluctantly around me, but the trousers remember—they hang in incriminating folds even before I zip them up. I have to hold my breath when I try to determine if what they know about me is bad. After all, they're my favorite trousers.

The first time I wore them was in the bar at Physical Culture, with Stephan, drinking scotch and soda in memory of someone—Stephan said his name, but I don't remember who it was. We were sitting by the window.

In a doorway across the street a bimboy (Stephan's word) in cut-off shorts was offering cartoon sketches for a dollar. On our side of the street a Rastafarian was doing the same thing, but charging five dollars a piece and getting it. We'd been there a long time, and bimboy hadn't sold anything, but he'd let a number of people pass through the doorway in which he and his goods were stationed. Stephan watched him and laughed between compressed lips, as if he might have latent gills fluttering in his neck.

"Business is booming," Stephan said, "whatever it is."

"How many pictures do you think he has?" I asked.

Stephan was game. "Oh, about twenty."

I winked. "What do you think he'd do if I went up and bought him out?"

Stephan's lips let loose a sputter of laughter and his face broke into a grin. He looked at me with admiration. "He'd shit in his pants."

I can't help smiling a little, from habit, remembering: I've been keeping a poison capsule of Stephan in a false tooth.

TUESDAY AFTERNOON

A TREE has planted itself in front of my door. I can see its swaying outline through the frosted glass.

"Hello! Are you home?"

Didn't I hear the bell?

My house has turned into a black hole, sucking in the good and the bad.

"Hello?" she calls.

I can hear her rustling around outside.

"Hey, if you're in there, I came to apologize. Would you open the door?"

So she's come to be polite. What does she expect me to say? She's giggling.

"I promise I won't lay a finger on you."

She's trying to be ambiguous. People like her say things with double meanings and don't mean either of them. If I open the door, I'll be humiliated, and if I don't, she'll think that she's gotten away with something. She'll realize later how obnoxious she was and consider herself lucky I wasn't home. Worse, if she thinks I'm not home, she might rant at the air, and then I'll never be able to look at her again. She's turning to go.

"Who is it? Just a minute."

This is going to be awful: she didn't hear me, only the door opening. She's halfway down the walkway, shading her eyes with one hand, but she can't see that I'm standing here, because the house is dark. I can't bring myself to say anything more. She looks like a fool, marching this way without any idea of who's waiting for her. She has that uneasy expression people get when they've discovered someone is watching them. Then, she looks relieved too soon—she's seen my face.

"Jesus, what happened to you?"

She has a lot of nerve, rousing someone out of their house, then demanding to know why they look so bad.

"I had an accident."

"Are you alright?"

"Yes—what are you doing here?" It sounds solicitous, but I can't help it. The worse it gets, the more polite I'll sound, so I'd better act happy to see her. "Come in, it's nice to see you."

"I was going to talk to you at work, but you weren't around, and the receptionist told me you were sick."

Good, she feels like she has to explain.

"Sit down."

She has to be herded to the sofa, because if she sits in my chair it's all over. It makes no difference, I know, but I have this momentary goal.

I perch on the edge of my easy chair, cocking my knees, looking spry. Now she can proceed.

"What happened?"

What happened? She's rustling again, and wants to point at my face.

"I wrecked my truck," I say. "Actually, I got rear-ended. I hit the windshield."

"Wow. Can I see it?"

I hesitate. "The truck?"

"Yes." She presses her fingers between the knees of her jeans.

"Alright. It's in the garage."

It would be out of line to ask why. Suburban people feel that they can come into your house and ask you anything they want, and it's you who is strange if you show any shock.

We've got to go through the kitchen, and I have to turn on the light in the garage: she's one of those people who like to gawk at accidents.

"In the back. The taillight's broken, otherwise it's not much. It still drives."

She frowns. Her face is dark and freckled and polished. Her features are so fine that if you were blind, you'd have to use a single finger to feel all the contours exactly, and it would take a long time; your lonely nose would probably pick up the lemony scent of furniture polish.

She smiles, bounces once on her heels, and seems satisfied. "My brother can fix that for you. I'll ask him tomorrow."

I must look astonished, because she's shaking her head and I think she's going to giggle again, but no, she's distracted by the way her matted, curly hair swings as she talks, and I'm afraid it will mesmerize her, and she'll close her eyes, and keep swinging her hair back and forth like that.

Finally she snatches it out of her face with one hand and we're going back into the house. I feel sorry for her hair, splaying out rigidly between her rough fingers. I can imagine her stuffing a mattress with those hands, with that hair.

I try to make no noise, following her into the living room. I wish we could just materialize in our places again, and I could sit in my easy chair before she speaks. She pinches her fingers between her knees once more, shrugs her shoulders, and looks at me deliberately.

"Anyway. I wanted to apologize for the other night, for hitting you—and for Sunday, too."

"It's not necessary to apologize." I touch my swollen face. "The windshield didn't."

She smiles. I made her feel better. "Well, you can punch your windshield back and no one would know."

How right you are.

"Listen, if there's anything I can do for you, maybe go to the store, pick up a prescription—have you been to a doctor?"

Temporary dread, because I'm really starting to believe that I wrecked my truck, and if I did and had been taken to a doctor, I wouldn't have gotten away with it so easily.

I shake my head. "I'm fine."

She seems put off, and I'm sure she thinks I want her to leave. I do, but I don't want her to think so. "Do you want a drink?"

Now she looks confused. "Alright."

I break for the kitchen. "Ice?"

"Yes"

My hand is in the freezer, but I'm interrupted by the thought of her at Marjorie's house, staring into the refrigerator. I poke the ice around in the glasses. Bourbon. Christ, it's Faye's bourbon, one of the two bottles she gave me to take home for "medicine." I hope Liann doesn't ask me what kind it is, because it's Faye's esoteric specialty and I wouldn't know how to account for it.

"Here."

"Thanks." She's gulped half of it. "Listen, I have to explain. I was crazy that night. My mother and I had just finished having a fight, and—when that happens—" She illustrates a mushroom cloud with her fist, somehow. "I was drinking pretty heavily, the way I was at the picnic. It usually calms me down. And—I know how this sounds—but it helps when I'm in pain. I don't know, when I saw you at the restaurant— you see, I know you're a friend of my mother's."

"I'm not really that friendly with your mother," I say. I don't know why I'm protesting, since I'll only have to explain myself further.

"Well, you drive her to work, so when I saw you in the restaurant, I knew that I'd have to smile, say 'how are you?,' and be nice, and I just couldn't do it. You see, it had nothing to do with you—"

She sets her bourbon down quickly, as if it no longer belongs to her, and is suddenly jolted by sobs.

I rise from my chair and move around the coffee table, descending beside her. I have to interrupt the sobs and lead her away from them before they fall into remorse. I don't know whether I should touch her with a finger or put an arm around her, but I must do something before she leans toward me because then it will be too late. I try to hold her up and not let her slump.

"Don't worry about your mother," I say, and it sounds conciliatory.

Her tears are gone, and I sigh (from relief). The hair brushes against my nose as she turns her head. Her face is damp, her lips are quivering, and she settles into an exhausted but happy smile.

"I watched you at the picnic," her voice is confidential and giddy, "from one of the upstairs windows. When I saw you head for the house, I hurried down." She shrugs. "You've been driving my mother to work since I was a kid. I always thought you were creepy—I mean, if I thought about you at all." She smiles apologetically. "But after what I did, I was worried that you might have told her, so I watched you. Then I was surprised, because at the picnic you seemed to be such a different person, as if you were walking through all those people in a daze. You were a long ways away."

"I was very much there," I say acidly, not appreciating the idea that I seemed like anything at all.

"Would you believe I don't really remember what I said to you? It was probably something bad. I get mad at people I want to impress, whether I've humiliated myself or not."

"I don't really remember what you said either."

She looks disappointed.

"Not that it wasn't bad, I'm sure that it was." I'm patronizing her, but she's stubborn enough to ignore it. She picks up her glass and finishes the drink.

"Do you have any more of this?"

"Lots."

"I'll get it."

She goes into the kitchen, and I'm left sitting in the middle of the sofa, wondering whether I should move to one end, return to my chair, or stay where I am—to no avail, since she's already back with the bottle in her hand, taking her place again.

"Just one more," she says, "then I'll have to leave. It's my lunch hour."

She's snuck her back into the corner of the couch and bent her knee, so that it's resting against my arm. I realize: I would be making an issue of it if I moved.

There's something warm and exuberant hovering around her, as if she wants everything and everyone to stay within reach—she's even glancing around the room, as if to draw in the walls like a blanket. There's a gentle smile on her lips.

(Stephan was grinning and smoking a cigarette and eyeing that bimboy as if he could unfurl his sticky lizard tongue and snap him up from across the street, and the sunshine was making our white shirts glare without warming them, and I was very sly and wise in that leisurely pause we had, before we had to shrug off the underworld, and knowing that was more delicious than.

WEDNESDAY AFTERNOON

THE *Handbook of Occupational Titles* is open on my desk. *Tends machine that cleans...*

Out on the factory floor, Liann's hands are describing their function, laboring with the switches and nozzles of her machine, filling and sating the limp, quilted skins that are laid out before her, then heaving up their heavy, unwieldy bodies. But first she beats them with a wooden pole. No wonder she is such a happy girl—if I went out of my office, down the hall, to the long window that overlooks the factory floor, I would see her alone making fierce, graceful gestures. While the others bent, hunkered, and gathered things in, she'd be raising her arms, arching her back, tightening her jaw, then letting the pole fly. I remember beating my car, and I know that these wild gestures can generate rage by themselves, in the friction of muscle sliding against muscle—become suddenly buoyant, quivering and tingling afterward. The memory is leaking into my upper arms like a fever—just when I'm thinking clearly about something as immediate as Liann's muscles, it's.

The perpetual incontinence of the brain. With me, memory is a sensual thing—a virus that hides in my spine and erupts under stress.

I need to get out of this office. I've never dared to panic here. But things are seeping into each other. First Stephan in my house, now Liann. Maybe this is what I was afraid of: my memory failing to keep things in order.

I have to get the payroll out before closing. All that's left for me to do is to tattoo the blank checks with the check-writing machine. I've done this thousands of times over the years, yet I still hold my breath as I pull down the lever and wait for the delicate crunching of needles inking the paper. I know exactly how much each person makes. I haven't looked at my own checks in years; they are automatically deposited.

There's a knock.

"Are the checks out, John?" It's the general manager, who likes to sign them himself.

"Two more to go, hold on." I wonder if he hears the miniscule sigh of each check when it's stamped.

He's sitting on my desk. "How's that eye?"

I touch it carefully with a finger. "It's alright."

"You're going to sue, aren't you?"

"Who would I—oh. No, it was a hit-and-run. Here you go."

There's a mousy knock on my open door. "John?"

We both look up at Liann.

"Oh, sorry."

The general manager slides his thigh off my desk and bows

to me, slaps the stack of checks against his palm, and lurches out past Liann, nodding to her. She's terrified, and I can't help smiling. She looks at the path of his departure in disgust.

"He doesn't like me. I went around with his son once, for a couple of months."

I don't know what this has to do with anything. I lean my elbows on the desk and glance down between them: *places cover over discharge tube and...*

Oh dear God. I look up and smile tentatively, crossing my arms over the page.

Now she's disconcerted. "We went to high school together," she explains.

I don't know which is worse, having her catch me with the occupational handbook or letting her think that I'm jealous of the general manager's son. I can't wait to subsume the last few gangly moments.

"I thought maybe I'd bring you over to my brother's garage, so he could take a look at your bumper."

I can't start meeting people indiscriminately like this, especially ones who know a lot about dents, at least not right now.

"I was thinking about leaving it the way it is. It isn't really that bad."

"You can't go around with a busted taillight. You'll get stopped all the time."

So I won't drive at night.

"And the body will rust where the paint's been scraped off," she pursues.

"I can get some spray paint," I say.

"What about the windshield?"

"Actually, I was thinking of buying a new one."

"What, a new windshield? Eddie can get you one for free at the junkyard."

"No, I mean a new truck." This conversation may cost me.

As it turns out: I am following Liann's car in my truck, wondering why I don't sneak a right turn when she goes through the next stoplight.

She turns right anyway. She has a Pinto wagon. There's a bunch of wood in the back, but I can see the top of her head. She's got her signal on now, in the middle of the block. There's a horrendous sprayed-concrete statue of a chef in a high white hat up ahead, then a row of shops. The backlit sign out front (under the chef's elbow) says there's a restaurant, a video store, a supermarket, an insurance company, a body shop, and a liquor store.

Liann honks, and that must be Eddie coming out of the garage. Liann leans out of her window and they both watch me drive in. They watch me get out, too.

"Eddie, this is John."

We shake hands.

"He drives Mom to work."

Eddie circles my car, bends down and feels the bumper. "Nasty," he says, squinting back at me, or rather at my eye.

I reach up and touch it. "It's alright."

"You should have seen it yesterday," Liann says.

"Shit," he says, shaking his head. "The body's okay. I can pound it back out. You want paint?"

72

"No," I say, "I don't think it's worth it."

"I can get you a new bumper, and I think I have a light that'll work."

"He needs a new windshield," Liann says, standing by my shoulder.

Eddie comes back around to look at the windshield. He touches that, too. "It's not so bad. If you're not going to bother with paint, you might as well skip the windshield, too."

He speaks in a volume that men mean to be ultrasonic, so that the women can't hear.

"Eddie!" Liann says.

"I didn't say I wouldn't do it," Eddie protests, unfortunately.

"I think you should skip it," I say.

Liann laughs shortly. "Give him the keys, John. Eddie, fix the window."

She thrusts her hand into my pocket and reaches for the keys. I'm too upset now to argue about anything.

"Tomorrow after five; okay, Eddie?" she says.

This is getting worse. These people are going to kidnap my truck.

"Baby, tomorrow is a maybe," Eddie chants, and Liann cuts him a fist in the air. The way she did it, the way he grinned—I think she must do that a lot. She gets in her car, and I suppose she means for me to get in it, too. Obediently, I fetch my things from the truck—jacket, and the *Handbook of Occupational Titles* (Why did I bring it in the first place?)—and follow her. I haven't ridden in the passenger's seat for as long as I care to remember; the last time must have been bad, because now I feel loathsome.

"Eddie likes to show off in front of me," Liann says, flashing her fingernails as she reaches for the keys and starts the car. The radio attacks me, but she shuts it off with one smooth gesture—keys to dial to wheel.

"What's that," she asks, "homework?"

"Huh? Oh." She points to the handbook in my lap. "Um, pleasure reading," I say lightly.

She makes an unnecessary circle around the parking lot—and wheels in before the liquor store.

"I'll be right back."

She runs into the store and returns in minutes, then shoves a pint of something in a brown paper bag into the glove compartment. The door to the compartment is resting very intimately on my knees, and I can feel the weight of her arm as she rummages through it to make room.

"Sorry," she says, patting my knees, one right after the other.

We're making an irrational circle in the parking lot again —for some reason, it's important to her that we leave the same way we came in. She looks at the grotesque chef statue but doesn't make a remark, and neither do I.

We're not far from my house, or Marjorie's either, for that matter. This meddlesome family is all around me, it seems.

"How did you get stuck driving my mother?" Liann asks, sounding ready to be amused. I wonder if she's forgotten about the summer I drove her, too. No, she's being coy.

I limit my response to a smile.

"Do you enjoy it?" she asks.

"How do you like living with her?"

Liann frowns but decides to let me get away with it. "Mom and I don't get along very well," she says. "I stay other places, whenever I can."

She pauses.

"She's alright, really. Sometimes I rag on her about everything she does—call her a fat, stupid bitch and tell her I hate her—but I know she doesn't mind as much as she makes out, even when she's wailing and waving her arms. She asks for it, so what else can I do, ignore her?"

She pauses again.

"I've got my wood shop in her garage, and I can't afford a place of my own with a garage. She charges me rent, too—by the square foot, do you believe it? It comes out to one hundred and thirty-seven dollars a month. She measured my bedroom on my eighteenth birthday—woke me up to do it, too."

The conversation is snowballing. "Why do you need a wood shop?" I ask in blind desperation.

She laughs again. "You're a trip."

This isn't going very well. But I have to think of something nice to say, because we've just arrived on my block. Good-bye-and-thank-you seems like a wobbly option.

She swings into my garage, and I hope that whatever lapse of sense has made her do this will pass before she drives through the back wall. Suddenly she stops and cuts the engine, and appears to be perfectly aware of the fact that she's parked her car in my garage. She picks up my hand—I think she meant to go for her purse, but she seems, after all, to be really having some sort of seizure.

"What's the matter?" she asks. She looks at me in surprise, because I've retrieved my hand, which I am holding myself to protect it from anyone else.

"Nothing."

She tries to shake her fingers playfully between my clenched hands.

"You can't touch me like that. I'm sorry, but you just can't."

"I thought you liked me. What's the matter, are you gay?"

"God, that's beside the point."

"Beside *what* point?" Liann folds her arms and glares out the window.

I can't find the door handle.

"Oh no you don't!" She's covered the distance across the seat and pinned my hand with hers. I slide my right eye over as far as I can, to continue looking for the handle. Her hair falls like a curtian of moss and blocks my view. "John, I'm twenty-five years old, and I won't tell my mother." She pulls away for a second. "You haven't been sleeping with my mother, have you?"

"Oh please, Liann."

She laughs. "Now, hold still."

Her lips move along my cheek, down my neck. Her hand slides up my thigh, almost, then presses hard. "Are you sure I'm wrong?"

I must have closed my eyes, because I'm opening them now—and something has changed; she's snuck her leg over mine, and her blouse is undone.

"Please don't touch me," I say quietly.

"I won't, I promise."

How do people get out of these situations? She's kissing me, and I can't do anything about it, as far as I can tell, without hurting her. What's she doing now? I can feel her hair against my face, she's looking down. This is horrible. "Don't do that. You were right before, I'm gay."

"Oh, yeah, sure." She laughs. "It's too late."

"Please."

"Shh. Shut up, will you?"

"Why are you doing this to me?"

That got her, she's staring at me now, with the most awful, lopsided smile working its way along her lips.

"No particular reason," she says, closing her eyes.

I'm sunk. I have a suspicion of what's happening under her skirt. How did she manage that?

Something has come into my throat, like a sob, and my eyes are blurred. Her eyes are wide, and she's examining my face in astonishment. I think I've just managed to convince her.

"I'm sorry," she whispers. She's holding very still. She looks scared. I'm sorry, too.

I slip my hands up under her shirt, round her trunk, and pull her toward me. Her slack lips press against my neck, her forehead falls to my shoulder, sadly. Her skin is smooth, hot and dry, her narrow back is round. My arms can circle all the way around her. I wonder if anyone has ever wanted to carve their initials into her heart, with an arrow through it. She lies morosely still, then sniffs. I don't have the strength to grope for the door handle, not directly, but I've never.

Run my hands down, under her arms, over her breast. She

77

catches her breath, and I can feel the twinge clear up inside her. She turns her face farther away from mine. Her hips start to move slowly, and I'm curiously calm as a shudder of anxiety wends its way through my skin, carelessly rubbing each cell into an uneven shiver.

I feel her body, uniform and perfect, one spot deceptively leading to the next. My hand is led over her knee, up her thigh, then impressed by the mysterious confluence of muscles and led away, passing over a lacelike, papery region of tissue before I reach her buttocks, which are cool, and I can feel the trail of heat leading me over and down, until the surfaces begin to race back to that point of temperature. My fingers dip into a cloud of steam, and I can't tell whether they're touching skin or air, and I close them around her, trying to resist the temptation to tear through handfuls of flesh to free my choking groin. Then I'm trembling, and stiffening to force the uneasy wave of hot.

I'm still, and so is she. The locks in my muscles have slipped. I take my hand away and smack it into the elusive door handle. She starts at the noise and raises her head, as if I've woken her up. She doesn't look at me, flicking her hair over her face like a veil. "Can we go inside?" she says.

I give the door handle a pull, and we fall out one way or another. I unlock the door to the kitchen, and Liann goes for the half-empty bottle of bourbon while I go for the glasses. Her shoes must have come off in the car, because she's walking barefoot into my living room.

WEDNESDAY NIGHT

She's sitting in the middle of the couch with her feet up on the coffee table. She looks as though she's just been caught in a downpour, her skirt wrinkled, her hair damp around the edges: bedraggled. Liann seems to feel the way she looks, because she's pouring a lot of bourbon into the glasses. I sit down next to her and put my feet on the coffee table. She drains her glass and pours another big one.

"That's better," she says to herself, but casts me a discomfited glance.

Which means that I must look worse.

"I've never really done that before," I say.

Liann reaches for the bottle impulsively, but she pours and swallows with deliberation.

"God," she says.

She pours again, a little less this time, sips, then rests the half-empty glass in her lap, rubbing the base of it with her thumb.

"I started fucking when I was thirteen," she says, taking my wrist and guiding the glass in my hand under the bottle. "It seemed like a good idea at the time. Then all holy hell broke loose. After that, I never said no, because that would have meant I was wrong in the first place. If I'd gone back on my word at that point, I would have had too much to regret. But you know, people talk, and it got out of hand. For a while."

I can't think of anything to say.

"I used to drink too much." She turns to me specifically. "I still do. I think we should get drunk together. You ought to see me that way."

"Why?"

"I don't know. Because I think"—she corrects herself—"I *hope* you wouldn't mind."

"Why would I mind?"

"I don't know. I just want to make sure—that I don't have to pretend to behave around you." She snorts. "After I hit you, I figured I didn't have anything to lose."

"I'd better have another drink," I say.

She laughs at this, and I hope the drinks will hit her very soon. She's pouring them stiff again, and I'd be grateful if she'd get completely plowed and possibly lose all memory.

"I like you too, Liann, but after this—I mean after we get drunk—you have to promise to keep away from me. It has nothing to do with you. I just can't manage it."

"You're not making sense," she says. She's one of those people who get very insistent when they're drunk. "Besides" —she winks luridly—"it's too late."

I must be turning red, because she giggles apologetically.

80

"You don't make a lot of sense yourself," I say. "Just take my word for it. It's important."

"What could be so important that you can't have a lover?"

"It isn't any of your business."

She's frowning comically, but her eyes are glittering. "Alright, it's none of my business. But I dare you to say that's how you really want it."

"I do."

She doesn't look as though she believes me, and her expression is making me laugh.

"It's true."

"Well then," she says, sliding a little closer, "prove it." She must be drunk now, because this is getting absurd.

"I'll be right back," I say, laying my hand briefly on her knee and going into the kitchen. I slip through the back door and into the garage, where her car door is still open. The interior light is shining on the bent cover of the *Handbook of Occupational Titles*. I slide it across the seat, shut the door, and the garage goes dark. I thumb through to page 774 on my way to the couch, smooth back the pages, and lay the heavy book in her lap. I pick up her index finger and place it down on entry number 780.685–014.

Liann marks the spot, folds over the cover to see what the book is, then looks at me curiously.

"Go ahead, read," I say.

"STUFFING MACHINE OPERATOR," she says out loud. She doesn't read very well, I can tell already. She gives me another curious look, then goes on. "Tends machine that cleans and fluffs filling and blows it into..." She leaves off reading aloud but continues to move her lips, sliding her finger along the column.

She finishes but keeps staring at the book, and moves her finger back to the beginning. She reminds me of Eddie, running his fingers along my dents and cracks—as if neither one of them trusted their eyes. She runs through the whole entry again, word for word.

"I don't get it," she says, more annoyed now than curious. I don't think she likes having people watch her read.

I take the book out of her lap and toss it on the coffee table, then take her hand. It doesn't look like a hand that beats mattresses, and I'm starting to think: she didn't seem to recognize the description in the book. Or perhaps she recognized it wrongly.

"It isn't you, Liann, it's the machine."

Her eyes cloud, and her hand leaps minutely within mine, like a little fish. I think she wants some whiskey. She frowns again and lowers her head slightly, so that her hair hangs.

"What?" she whispers.

I'm not going to say it again. I look at her hand, imagining how badly she wants it back. It's perfectly still, but that could mean a lot of things. I have to let it go anyway, because even if she doesn't want her drink, I want mine.

"Don't you see, it isn't you I'm interested in—like that."

She lets me take a long hit before she speaks.

"I don't think I understand."

Actually, I was hoping she'd be content with some amount of confusion.

She folds her arms across her chest and glares across the

room, much as she had before, in the car, when I tried to explain—but I'm learning not to put too much faith in her attitudes. Her attention seems to drift off, and her eyes float up to the corner of the room, over the bookcase, to the door, to the hallway.

"I'll be right back," she says.

I see a sliver of light come and go as she opens the bathroom door. I hope she isn't going to break anything. The toilet flushes, and she comes back out. Her sly smile has returned.

"Okay, let's go."

"Where?"

"You know where, come on. Bring the bottle." She doesn't wait, but goes straight through the kitchen door.

She's in the car, clear over in the driver's seat, and the only way I can talk to her is to get in.

"Listen—"

"Close the door."

I have to, because she's let out the emergency brake and we're rolling back. She kicks in the engine before we hit the street.

"Where are we going?"

"Well, I don't exactly keep one of those things at home."

"Don't be angry. Let's just stop. I shouldn't have said anything to you. It isn't true anyway, not really, not the way you think—I only wanted to convince you."

"Cold feet?" She stops at an intersection and smiles at me sideways. I don't think she's insulted. My God, she's happy. She thinks it's a lark.

"Relax." She turns on the radio full blast, to shut me up. When we're a block from the front gate, she cuts the music. "Follow my lead, alright?"

She takes the bottle from me, and the slam of her door is very loud from in here. She's forgotten to douse the head-lights, and the beam makes the back of her skirt and her calves glow. The image is strangely violent and gives me a shrinking feeling. I stretch for the knob, push it in, and she dissolves into black shadow, turning around toward me. I slide out of the car.

"Liann, wait."

She shakes her head, so that her hair swishes from side to side. I catch up with her just as she slips one set of bare toes into the cyclone fencing and hoists herself up and over.

She smiles at me through the fence. "Your turn."

"I don't think I can do that."

She puts her hands on her hips, the whiskey bottle jutting out from her fist. "No, I guess not. Just a minute."

She prances over to the gate, into the guard's booth, takes a key off a hook, and unlocks the gate. I would object, but she'd be in a lot of trouble if someone came back and found us arguing here, so I slip through. We could get arrested. I could be strip searched, and that would be bad. I should per-manently bond my clothes to my incriminating skin, if it isn't too late already.

Liann grabs my hand roughly and pulls me toward the building, back to the side wall, between the warehouse next door and under the row of office windows. She points with her finger at the first window, then the next, counting them off just the way she reads—she stops at five.

"That's your office, isn't it?"

I have no idea, but she says it is.

"Give me a boost." She puts the bottle down and laces her fingers together into a stirrup. "Like this."

"Liann."

"Don't be a jerk, come on."

I do it, and now she's up there looking down at me through the window. "Wait," she says, and comes back with my chair. I don't know how she expects to help me up with a chair.

"Stand on this," she says and drops it to the ground.

I stand on the chair and pull myself through the window. I guess the chair is going to stay outside.

Liann moves in slow motion over to the door and pokes her head into the corridor. I start to creep up behind her, but she collides with me on her way back and my hand bumps into the check-writing machine. The little wheeled table it sits on skids and smacks into the wall. She reaches over to my desk and grabs the whiskey bottle by the neck, and I think: I've never seen anyone so violent about wanting a drink. Liann is standing by the door, and I find myself crouching under my desk.

I've been here before, but it looks different in the dark. I recognize a water stain in the unvarnished wood, and realize that I feel a lot better right now, no matter what, than I did the last time I saw it: it was lunchtime, and I hadn't wanted to go out, so I climbed under my desk and hid there. After fifteen minutes I thought someone might spot the shadow of my shoes, but I didn't dare come out until everyone had gone back to their offices. That was much worse than this.

It's a very fast, remote thought, and I'm peeking out, around the corner of my desk, trying to find Liann. The night guard walks past my door; his trailing foot is about to disappear. Liann steps out into the hall and cracks him in the nape of the neck with the whiskey bottle. He falls, but her swing carries through and lands the bottle against the door frame, where it shatters. She stands very still; the bottleneck slides through her fingers and clinks to the floor. She shakes her head.

"Do you have a key to your office?" she asks.

I'm on my feet, next to the desk. "Yes."

"We'd better lock him in."

She's disappeared down the hall. The guard's feet pass the door, followed by his body, then Liann. She swings him around and drags him inside.

"He's okay. We ought to be gone before he wakes up, though," she says, running down the hall once more.

I lock the door, and jog to the end of the corridor, where I can see her striding quickly across the factory floor. I follow her down.

She goes to the machine, cuts her path, and circles to the place where she stands every day. She stops and gives it a blank stare, then glides her eyes over the lever, the toggle switch, and the dial on the scale. She narrows her eyes on the hopper, down the discharge tube, then back up the hopper. She waits for me to come up beside her, then flips up the toggle. The machine croaks, then hums. She guides my eyes with hers up the hopper, hits a switch, and looks at the scale.

"If you don't hit this weight"—she points to a taped-off mark on the dial of the scale—"it doesn't matter, because you can throw this"—she points to the lever—"and it'll go through. The blower is timed to fill a cover in three minutes. It has an automatic weight that gives a signal, but use the manual switch if you want. The pole is right there." She points to the wooden rod held up in a sling.

She hesitates, as if there were something she was holding back, then: "The sewing needle is there. Use the foot pedal to start it, and it'll run through the plate. You have to hoist the mattress up to it. There are—" She begins, then pulls a rectangle of limp batting off a dolly. "The guys were ahead of me today, there are some covers left over. I'll put one on the table for you, then you're on your own."

I think she expects me to stuff a mattress.

"I'm going back to the car. I'll leave the padlock open for you. I'll wait half an hour, then I'm going, okay?"

I feel like a boy with his hands in his pockets, getting contraceptive advice from his father.

Liann hasn't shown me the joint of her left middle finger, where it got caught in the hopper that summer, and it's hard to tell now. But I remember when it happened, because I had to type the insurance forms, and I remember that she didn't cry—they took her outside and she sat on a crate with a whole choir of people around her. The crates were like risers, and everyone who lined up was moaning and cooing, and straining for a better look. The sight made me think of Physical Culture.

"I'll see you soon," she says and steps up to me quickly.

She moves her hand with the scarred finger up around my face and her tongue flickers against my ear. She puts her hand under my jacket and runs it up my back, where I'm sure she can feel the irregularities, then pushes me back against the table of the machine. Her other hand has flipped the blower toggle, and I can feel the misdirected gust of air lift the hair on the back of my head.

She's walking away, and the blower keeps lifting my hair, like a gentle hand. Liann's finger was cut to the bone; I remember Marjorie telling me about it on the way to work the next day—about seeing the bone of her own flesh and blood, how it split right open, clean and white, just like you'd think. How the doctor injected the torn flesh with novocaine, right into the bloody, ripped part because it was so deep.

The machine is humming, vibrating against my hip where I'm leaning against it. I climb up on the platform and lie on top of the billowing mattress. My groin feels as if it's been dipped in ice water. The corner of the mattress blows over my shoulder; fabric flutters around my ankles.

I hold the flap of batting off my shoulder and roll over onto my stomach. I don't know where to distribute myself. I won't fit in the hopper; the jam mechanism would shut it off instantly. That was her idea, anyway. It's absurd.

I look up at the suspended pole, trying to imagine its impact—but the dull wooden rod refuses my attention, nothing. I follow the line of the pole with my eyes, down and along its oily length, looking for a shape that will reveal the machine's intentions.

I can't even remember the description in the handbook—

this machine doesn't seem to admit to it, anyway. This isn't what I meant: it's not so trivial. I should never have allowed this to happen—there are some places one should never go, and not for the usual reasons.

The hopper shuts down abruptly, and the blower, It's very quiet; the machine and I are at a loss, in a silent stupor.

I'm beginning to grow—bored.

I scramble to the ground, stumble—and my heel skips off a resilient flange of metal. A rapid clattering discharges behind me. The bullets of sound ricochet off the concrete walls, until they sink into my flesh and this cold, gritty cavern is dull with silence once more.

Without looking around, I press the pedal again—deliberately this time. My ankle is hot where I twisted it, but hotter where my sole lies upon the tense, fibrillating metal. The needle pumps the air in burning droplets of sound, ululating in a catastrophic mathematics of pain, stiffening inward, like an electrocution.

My foot slips from the pedal. I hadn't counted on this. Folding my arms over the edge of the platform, I retch. Bile and whiskey spill between my lips.

For a moment I think I have evacuated myself, and I move carefully, shaking my legs. My trousers are all wet. The needle has pierced every pore, drawing transparent blood and leaving me so deeply cold that my muscles ache in knots. I am shuddering in a noxious daze in the wake of the needle's spasm. The metal shelf under my elbows feels mushy.

Slowly, my head feels light. Pinpricks of darkness swim before my eyes; I turn and look upon the needle.

It sits, poised above the slotted metal plate, unthreaded—and patient beyond any human standard of desire. Without purpose, insensible of sewing or tearing, it is utterly selfless—and that is the threat.

I rip the mattress cover off the table and shove it back into the bin where she took it from, then shut down all the switches. I can feel the presence of the needle behind me as I walk away.

I don't know how to get out of here. The door to the factory floor is open—where the guard came in for his rounds—and it's a shallow angle to the gate.

Liann's left the padlock open, but she's slipped in the bar so that it's resting just short of the teeth.

She's sitting in the car, waiting for me, drinking from the bottle she had in the glove compartment.

"Alright, let's go," I say, not sure what I mean by this.

"Yessir," she says.

The engine flares, and Liann squirms to attention. She smiles, and I don't know whether it's because of me or the car.

"I put the cover back in the bin," I say.

"Chicken out?" she asks.

She has no idea what she's talking about. I think she knows as much as she wants to know, or has simply lost her curiosity in the flow of alcohol.

"You know what?" she says. "I'm tired. I feel as though I've just gotten off work." She laughs uncomfortably. "Well, John, it's been one hell of an evening."

I hope she doesn't mean to drop me off at my house, because I can't, just yet, let her out of my sight, not after all she's found out about me.

I'm very glad she's swinging into my driveway. It looks so ordinary and familiar. I've got the door handle down pat, but she's already climbed out on her side and is heading toward the kitchen door. I follow her inside.

But I am not prepared for this: there's a pan of cold ravioli on the stove.

I put my hand on her wrist to let her know she should wait, then I think she might leave, and close my fingers around her. We see Stephan passed out on the couch. The other bottle of Faye's bourbon has been tapped, and one of our glasses (mine) is half full.

Liann gives me a questioning look, and I shake my head violently enough to elicit silence. I drag her off to my room, close the door, and turn on the light.

"It's alright," I say. "He's a friend of mine from the city."

Liann shrugs and turns away, slithering her shoulders out of her blouse before she has the buttons quite undone. I turn out the light. I don't hear anything from her, then I see her back emerge grayly from the shadows. I cross the room to the window that faces the backyard and lower the blinds. I can hear her drop things on the floor and the static of sheets separating.

"I can't see you at all," she says.

"Leave the light out. I don't want you to look at me," I say, too urgently. I hesitate. "Please."

"Alright," she says wearily. "Come here."

She's in my bed already. I can hear the disturbed sheets

rustling around her, and I hope they can make that same smooth sound around me, disguising each of my scars with a husky flutter. I can't say a word to her, even when she asks where I am and is slightly afraid of my silence in the dark. Her fear is in fun—a mixed-up remnant from a horror movie, a shred of fabric caught in the machinery.

I slip my hand into the dresser drawer and pull out pajamas, the new ones that are still thick and stiff. I'm quick about it so she won't notice, or at least I can delay her noticing. I feel heat against my chest as I move toward the bed and lift my corner of the covers, a heat I've been mistaking for fear—but I can't know it for anything else because I haven't had time to think it through.

Her hands are warm against me, through the cotton of my pajamas and the mud of my skin. I lean my clean face against her neck but cringe in pain—my face is muddy now, too. I don't have anything to give her, except my cool, toneless feet, and my insensible hands—my hands are so disturbed I can't feel her between them. She smells like dead oak leaves, as if she's just stood on my bed in the dark, shedding them slowly —leaves that have lived less than a year, then fired up again and spun away to the ground, where they've already begun to fester into a virile, hectic stink. It brings Stephan to mind, with his lawn mower grumblings, and I'm afraid he might rumble in and chop her up into soft, warm loam at any moment.

"I can't bear to have you touch me."

I have slipped my words between the gentle sounds of the bedclothes, trying to make them inconspicuous. I'm holding her hands. I put her at arm's length and let my wrist train across her waist. She can't read my wrist from that remote valley of skin, or even with her fingers, because she's probably unfamiliar with the words that are carved there. I'm reading her face with the fingers of my other hand, feeling her lips spread reluctantly into sleep.

LATER WEDNESDAY NIGHT

I CAN'T sleep. I've been concentrating on removing my arm from Liann's side, but she turned in her sleep and I jumped out, so now.

I'm dealing with the doorknob, quietly. I had wanted to get up and pace around the house, but I just remembered that Stephan is (or was) sleeping on the couch.

Most people look younger when they're sleeping, but not Stephan. He looks older, about Liann's age. But then, he must be twenty-five by now. I think he once told me he's Austrian, but it seems, after all, as if his country of origin were just an ordinary neighborhood of no particular nation. Looking at him, I reluctantly wonder if his mystery might be nothing but contrivance. There's nothing alien about him—wherever he's from, it's too small a place to have anything *but* an accent.

"Stephan," I say. I don't know which part of him to shake to wake him up. I don't want him to hit me. I pull a book off the shelf and throw it at him. Only his eyelids move.

"John," he says, and a lethargic hand reaches for the book. He squints at the title, then puts it on the coffee table. I didn't try to choose an appropriate volume, but I recognize it from the binding: it's a thesaurus.

"What are you doing here?"

Stephan sits up and runs his hand through his hair. He lets out a deep sigh.

"It's a hell of a long way out here," Stephan says, as if he were reprimanding me.

"It's supposed to be," I answer.

Stephan wiggles his eyebrows to throw off the sleep and looks over at the whiskey bottle. He picks it up and reads the label, trying to remember where he's seen it before. If he figures it out, I might have to start making excuses, so:

"I saw Faye the other night."

"Faye?" He rolls his eyes. "So how is she? That means you were in the city. Why didn't you call me?"

"I went there to look for you. She's fine. I think I helped her along a little. She knows what she wants now. You should be kept abreast of these things, I guess. She's a bruiser." I pointed to my mangled eye.

He looks at it, whistles, and shakes his head. "What's the deal?"

"You know what she's like," I say. "I said something she didn't want to hear, and she started swinging. It worked out fine, at least for her. You might want to follow it up. You could send her some girls to drag around by the hair or something."

"What about you?" Stephan asks.

"I'm retired, remember?"

"I mean, how did you handle it?" He points specifically at my eye, then suddenly: "You were looking for me?"

I curl into my easy chair and nestle my head against its wing. "I think so," I say weakly. "I was scared. Why did you come here—before?"

Stephan stares at his hands, preparing an answer, and right away I don't want to hear it.

I wave my hand. "It's been a hard week, that's all. There's this girl who keeps harassing me. First she hits me, then she takes away my truck, then she—forces herself on me. In fact, she's in the bedroom right now, dead asleep. We just broke into the factory where I work, which was also her idea, and I'm not sure, but I think we may have injured someone. It's gotten to the point where I—" I stammer, squeeze my eyes shut (briefly, because it hurts), and take a deep breath. "I think I was actually happy to see you when I walked in the door."

Stephan snorts. "She's the girl you told me about?"

"What? Yes. I forgot about that. I thought I was inventing it then. No, I *was* making it up. But now it seems as if I'm the only one who thinks so."

Stephan turns with great effort and hooks his bare heels over the arm of the couch. He locks his hands behind his head and starts doing sit-ups.

"I don't know a lot about factory girls," he says. "I have to work this liquor out of my bones, you don't mind, do you?"

I'm sure I haven't given him an adequate explanation of

*

Liann, and I can't believe he's content with such a slim and jarring account—but then, he may not know any better when it comes to ordinary people and what one would normally expect from them.

"Did you take anything?" Stephan asks.

"Mattresses," I say facetiously.

Stephan pauses in the middle of a sit-up, then goes on. "Alright, you don't have to tell me," he says. "But this house gives me the creeps. It looks as if it's never been used."

"It hasn't," I say, thinking about how long I've lived here, counting back.

Stephan finishes doing his sit-ups and turns toward me. "The bathroom smells like a motel," he says, grimacing as if at some sleazy antiseptic odor. "How can you live this way?"

"Stephan, I moved into this house when you were three years old," I say sharply. "Did you come here to offer decorating tips?"

"Why did you stop coming around?" Stephan asks.

When I don't answer, he continues, "I want to know. I thought, a few months, fine, he's cooling it for a while, but it's been a long time and I thought you might be angry with me. We used to be friends."

I still don't say anything.

He reaches into his back pocket and throws a roll of bills onto the coffee table. "I brought the money I borrowed, if that's it."

I don't know what to say. Borrowed—this is new to me. Slowly, I reach for the wad of cash, heft it in my hand, and put it down again.

"You could have at least told me you were leaving," Stephan says. "Didn't you think I'd wonder what happened? I kept trying to think of what I'd done to piss you off. Then, when I never ran into you or heard anyone talking about you anymore, I realized you weren't around town, and that you weren't just avoiding me—then I got worried. I had to come and see for myself. Even after the way you hustled me out of here on Sunday, I had to come back and find out."

Stephan's circular words are turning me around and around on a lathe, shearing off particles and transforming them into nothing but a dry, burnt odor. I can't trust it, this surface friction that is wearing me down into a thing that yields to his manipulation. It would be so easy to give in to him, to listen to his words, to be transfixed by what he has not said—what he doesn't know. And to be caught, in the end, lulled and captured by his will to understand and make me over.

"I stopped coming for a reason," I say quickly, remembering the last day I spent in the city, a year ago. It resides in my memory like an unwelcome sore, the surrounding tissues silently abiding a dull ache. I have learned to resist probing it.

Stephan gazes at me, respectfully.

I don't remember the introduction itself—just Stephan, the man named Bill, and me seated at a table in the bar area. Bill was sweaty from the weight room, his damp tank top a slightly grayer shade than his skin. An old scar looped around his collarbone.

"Where did you get that necklace?" Stephan asked.

Bill grinned. "I wore out one head, and had a transplant," he said, laughing hard.

Bill's voice was loud, and clearly he relished the fact that everyone in the bar had heard his joke. I glanced sharply at Stephan, but his eyes were full of irrepressible merriment. I couldn't believe he would be so indiscreet.

"Stephano," Bill drawled, without taking his eyes from mine, "would you run over and grab me another gin?"

Behind Bill's chair, Stephan rolled his eyes at me and winked. "Want anything, John?"

I shook my head.

"That's my boy," Bill called after him.

I was appalled.

"Thanks, kiddo," Bill said when Stephan handed him the gin. He tasted it, smacked his lips, and set it down again. "Needs a little spice."

He snatched up my hand in his, turned it palm up, and as the bar settled into a stunned silence, I saw that he held a switchblade in his other hand. I couldn't bear to look at Stephan; I didn't want to know how much of this had been planned, whether it was cruelty or profit or stupidity that had brought him to such a petty form of betrayal. My elbow was twisted at an impossible angle, and the pain left me incapable of speech. I'm sure Bill saw it, but there was nothing I could do. The pressure on my hand continued to build, and I was afraid he would squeeze me like a sausage from its casing, leaving nothing but a heap of empty clothes on the seat of my chair. The blade hovered, then flashed downward, and nicked a flap of skin on my fingertip. Bill guided the wound over his gin glass, waited for a drop of blood to fall, then stirred the liquid into a rosy shade of pink with his blade, and downed it. "The spice of life," he said, and roared with laughter.

Bill released my hand and stood. I heard him slap me on the back, although I didn't feel a thing, as if my nerves had recoiled from the surface in horror. I stared into his smug, hateful face. "I'll see you," he said and walked away.

"Bye, Bill," Stephan called. Stephan looked at me and laughed nervously. His face was flushed, and I knew then that he had been afraid. The unused adrenaline was making him giddy with relief.

But I was not relieved—somehow it didn't matter if Stephan had acted out of cruelty or ignorance—yet I laughed anyway. I remember that. My only other choice was to expose myself.

Stephan's face had been flushed with grateful laughter. "You should have seen your face," he'd said in gasps.

Now, in my living room, his face is openly curious—but I can't help thinking he's got something on me, and perhaps he doesn't even know it.

"Was it something I did?" Stephan asks.

I shake my head. "No. It had nothing to do with you." I can feel tears of frustration swelling, about to spill over.

"I lost my nerve," I say quickly.

It's true, but I feel as if I've uttered an unforgivable lie. It may be true, but it's far from enough.

Stephan is impatient. "That's your business," he says dismissively, and searches me for more.

"That's all," I say helplessly.

"But I don't understand," he says crossly.

"Neither do I."

Stephan looks at me hard, then purses his lips. "I don't understand what happened. You had your thing, but you were cool. Nothing showed on you—you just did what you had to do and kept it to yourself."

"Kept it to myself," I repeat. "Then what are *you* doing here?"

Stephan looks aghast. His silent face is trying to fix an expression, and already I can see that it'll be one of guilt—in a moment his face will reveal only what he knows. But I don't even need to wait for it, because now I remember:

The blood from my finger had dripped all over my trousers. "Come up to my room and I'll give you something to change into," Stephan said. "I can't," I answered flatly. Stephan shrugged. "I'll bring down some clothes and meet you in the locker room, then." "No," I said, with a forced laugh. "Not now." Stephan rolled his eyes. "Oh come on, you're a legend in there, you know."

I never went back.

"Stephan," I say, "this has all been a complete misunderstanding. From the very beginning."

Stephan seems skeptical. He believes I am giving him the brush-off again. But there's really nothing I can do about that. Some things can't be spoken of: once they've passed, they are over. There's so much Stephan doesn't know—so much he clearly never wanted to know—that now it is much too late.

"I made a mistake," I say quietly. "That's all—really."

"I don't want to bring you any trouble." He nods in the

direction of the bedroom. "I just wanted to check you out."

"You didn't bring me any trouble," I say, meaning it, because it's all my own fault, and I could never show Stephan how much trouble he so willingly brought me in the past.

Still, I'm touched. It's a strange, sweet, but nauseous feeling, almost like: decay. I think that if my nose weren't full of tears, I'd be able to smell my petrified corpse beginning to rot at last.

I'd like to tell him to keep the money, but I think it would sound as if I were trying to get rid of him, which is really what I ought to do. "I'm sorry," I say instead.

"So am I," Stephan answers with the same note of grudging finality. He knows that he can't stay, and that I can't accommodate him.

"You don't have to leave tonight," I say, as he begins to rise. "I'm not kicking you out. Please, sleep on the couch."

I stand, shakily, giving him a look that is supposed to convey a delicate mixture of sympathy and determination, then turn away.

"Good night," Stephan says softly.

I nod, and teeter back to my room.

Slowly I ease the door closed, and still the latch seems to fall with a clang. But Liann doesn't stir.

I feel sore all over. My head aches, a soft and cozy kind of pain, like a horrendous wound felt through a romantic haze of morphine. I can hear her breathing. The sound fills me with longing, but I'm not sure for what; it might be for my own sleep. I feel very lonely, exhausted, and since I can't see anything, it's only the ache that defines my human shape. I'm about to go into the bathroom but stop in futility, and lean against the bathroom door, wrapping my arms around my body. The tenderness of my own gesture makes my eyes water again. A word, please, just a kind word whispered in the dark.

When I was nine, my cousin came upon me sitting in a closet with the door closed. I told him I was looking for a pair of shoes and thought I could find them better by climbing inside, then the door fell shut. The truth is, I'd gone into the closet with a hammer to smash my finger, but after he found me, I had to leave the hammer behind. It was a holiday, and the house was so full of people that I'd begun to shake, trying to hold still in my chair and smile. They all seemed to know how to display themselves, a family full of wits and buffoons and practical jokers enjoying the hideousness of the day. I wondered why my body felt uncomfortable, as if I were clanking around in a suit of armor. That's why I got the hammer. I never knew whether anyone had found it and figured out what I had been planning to do. (If you put a cat in the middle of a pool of water, on a brick just big enough for it to sit on but not lie down, the cat will never fall asleep, because every time it does, the touch of water on its fur will jerk it awake. Within twenty-four hours the cat will begin to hallucinate. Permanently.) For three weeks I trembled like a wet cat. Every time I thought about the hammer in the closet, I'd put my hands over my closed eyes, and hold my sphincter tight, thinking these things would keep people from discovering me —and if I squeezed hard enough, even I would cease to remember. Then one night I snapped. I went down to the

103

basement and smashed my thumb with a new hammer. I told my mother I'd gotten it caught in a door. For as long as my thumb throbbed, I didn't think about people knowing anything about me. I was in too much pain to care.

Practical jokes. When I was very small, I used to like to look at the scar my father had on his stomach. He caught me staring at it once, as he sat in the kitchen in nothing but his pajama bottoms, and gave me a long, assessing look as he rubbed the length of the scar. I wanted him to say something, but I also knew what to expect. "You know what this is, don't you?" he asked me in a stern voice. My mother giggled for no reason. His voice was always stern, and I could never tell when he was joking and when he was not. "That's where you came out of," he said. The two of them roared with laughter, and I stood there, wishing they would stop, wishing I were sharp enough to play along, but was never anything but flustered and harassed by their bitter jokes. The most obscene, embarrassing thing in the world, I thought then, and for a long time afterward, was laughter.

Years later I made tiny razor slits inside my armpits, where the sting of sweat would remind me—relieve me—for days. I could be anywhere and the pain would come on, like a small voice of my own, talking to me in its sharp little tongue. I'd been accused of being lonely so many times that when I felt the sting, I no longer felt awkward because of it—it was my own portable, irrevocable privacy. As the scars began to show up, I could even invoke my private isolation by rubbing my fingers idly under my shirtsleeves, tracing the welts.

When I first undressed in front of a sadist and exposed my harried skin to him, I was afraid, not of what he was about to do to me, but of what he would *think*—until I realized that he, too, was held wholly captive within himself. For the first time in my life, I felt at ease, trusting my own opacity, able to range freely through the landscape of the room. I remember thinking: this must be how normal people feel all the time.

I've splattered every evil thought I've ever had across my naked body, but in the end it's more cryptic than if I'd simply pushed them to the back of my mind. And that's what I've always accomplished: memory engineering. I don't remember my mother's maiden name, or how I learned to read, or what my father actually resembled under his steel-gray helmet of hair (I used to watch him chew!), and sometimes I even forget that they're dead. It's all reduced to mud. I've been working for twenty-five years, and now I don't even know if I remember them or not, because everything is exactly the same as it ever was.

The walls of my bedroom have grown transparent in the dark, and through them I can see: the mud flats roiling and bubbling, far into the light, and I am awed by their black volume.

Perhaps she doesn't have to know. If the room is dark, if I tell her not to be afraid, if I explain, carefully, that I was the victim of.

"Liann?" I whisper.

She turns in the bed, I can hear her, but she doesn't awaken.

"Liann?" I whisper again.

"Huh?" she says in a tiny, sleepy voice. "Where are you? Come here."

"Yes. Just a minute." I unbutton my pajamas and step out

of them. The air feels cool because my skin is flushed.

I may have to say a lot of things between here and the bed, but I can't move.

There's a loud clunk in the living room. Liann starts, takes in a gulp of air and holds it. I wait—and this time, my very skin appears to be shrinking, as if it had anywhere to hide. I grab hold of the knob to the bathroom door, ready to flee, yet again it is quiet. Liann breathes, and I can hear her head relax back into the pillow.

But the sound echoes in my inner ear, unbalancing me, and for a moment I'm thrown back to the sound that Stephan made days ago, pounding on my front door. Coming to see what had happened to me—what did he say? *When I never heard anyone talking about you.*

There are footsteps in the hall, coming toward the bedroom, hesitating there, on the other side of the door.

"It's that guy, right?" Liann says.

I hear her, but at the same moment it's there—the needle of fear, its blind, unthreaded eye piercing me again and again, and I—remember now:

You're a legend.

(Yes, now Stephan is turning the doorknob.)

All those men, for years. The ones I had been with—they had spoken of me, to others. I was known, even to people I had never met.

The door opens, and a narrow shaft of light spills in from the hallway, where I can see Stephan's profile.

"John?"

My privacy is not real. My hand is on the knob to the bathroom door. I can't move.

"Hey!" Liann says crossly.

I'm paralyzed. I made it all up. I look down at the pale, narrow shaft of light that is falling on my thigh. I've never seen this leg before—it doesn't look like anything I could move through an act of will. Others have seen it.

"John?" someone says.

I drop my hand from the door. Stephan gropes along the wall, and flips the switch.

I can see the two of them, am still seeing them, just as they were when the light came on.

Liann is screaming. But in the picture I have in my head, she's not screaming yet, just sitting up, blinking, open-mouthed.

Now Stephan is taking one step into the room, stopping. Liann is holding her fist to her lips. Stephan—Stephan is looking now, straining to keep his eyes from flight. I'm grateful to him for trying.

Liann has buried her head in her hands, and I'm afraid she will start to sob. But her voice, when it comes out, and her eyes, when they flash up, are angry.

"God! How could you be so stupid!" she spits contemptuously.

Stephan's eyes grab mine and hold them, telling me not to listen to her. He is motionless, standing there rock hard and steady, as if he knows that I could fall apart like an overcooked chicken at the slightest twitch. And that gives me the strength to turn my head, reach for my robe, and cover myself. When I turn back he is still there, but his eyes have grown full and red.

THURSDAY MORNING

THE room is dark except for the red-lit numerals on the digital clock: 7:23 A.M.. There's a price tag stapled to the sleeve of my pajamas, which makes me wonder, in an unconnected, transitory way, what kind of violation I have suffered in the night. For you, such a question might be posed in disgust. You'd worry that you might have laughed too loudly or grown misty in your drunkenness, or that you might be in someone else's bed. For me, it's a yearning for that part of the debauch that deteriorates most quickly—the moment when all forms of meaning are hinged, the cusp of this world, and then.

The nightmare: *your teeth fall out, your hair grows thin, and you change from a fencepost into your fifth-grade teacher, and the progression is just as predictable as the sun hurtling through an empty universe—your decline burns brilliantly, with a smoldering dread that has no hope, only a queasiness akin to vertigo, almost pain.*

But it's not like that now; I'm finding only a chain of visions —dry, sharp, and motionless, brightly lit: the factory, Liann, Stephan. A handsome young man and a naked girl, sitting, the two of them, on my bed. Where was I? I see them frame by frame, flipping into a long, internal documentary.

But I already know its essence. I'm awake, and there are things that I have to wake up to—so it doesn't feel as if anything has happened. No, I know what has happened, but I am still alive, and that amazes me. I have always cherished a particular fear—that knowledge could destroy the physical world in the absence of caution—but I am here, living proof of the graceless elasticity of consciousness. I can't tell yet whether or not I'm disappointed.

I'm a little hung over, but so comfortable that I feel compelled to rise, just to keep this moment from being sated. Have I changed?—I wonder suddenly. The thought is appallingly arbitrary. I'm not even sure where it's come from— whether it's the hemophilic ocean of my secret life, or the box of this suburban world.

Perhaps the answer is simple: yes, I have changed, but only enough to ask the question.

My ideas are becoming more trivial as they grow more complete, until all I have left is a glorified, elegant abstraction. As far as the world is concerned, I have kept quiet. My only failing has been: the spores of my deprecation, kept dank and dark for so long, have sprouted on my skin like mushrooms.

There were people here last night, and perhaps they're still here, somewhere in my house.

I must get up and move beyond the bedroom, and into the daylight. The living room is empty of evidence: no whiskey bottles, glasses, cigarettes, Liann's purse. There's motion in the air, and a chilly, sweet smell. The morning is delicate and headstrong, full of itself—I can feel time gathering on its haunches, preparing for a tremendous leap.

There is certainly no one here. A glance into the clean kitchen affirms that they too must have felt the surge of energy in the crisp morning, and sprung free of the house and my desperation. Liann, I suppose, straightened up the house, having found Stephan long gone. She is now bustling off to work, while he's hustling his way back across the bay. By the time they reach their destinations, the previous night will have buckled over into some irretrievable realm. Which must be why I feel so calm.

Liann's wrath, Stephan's sadness: neither one describes me—I have been so afraid of discovery that I never thought to fear its opposite, that I would simply be mistaken for something else. It is time now, now that I'm alone.

I haven't looked at myself in the mirror for a long time. I don't trust my eyes: they have never been used for this purpose. I believed if I did this, they would curl and sever each shaft of light into a random bouquet of useless and disorderly images, that my nudity would meet a stunned, quiescent eye and I'd have only a memory transposed from some other circumstance. I'd look long and hard, yet remain ignorant to the end. Perhaps now, before this time of safety slips away, I should see for myself. I shed my clothing.

Before the bathroom mirror, I search my tanned face for a

path leading downward, but there is no connection, only a luminous, pale glow at the base of my vision, and I must make the precipitous drop.

There. My eyes fall, then bounce away, settle again, skitter off and back, passing through a thin layer of relief so quickly they burn and fall to rest, lapped cool by tiny waves of amazement.

Next to the dead leaves that are my hands and the knotty, freckled knob of my head, the skin of my body is succulent, as if I could break open my chest and drink freshly from it. Beneath the knots and whorls of raised flesh, the worm trails of scar tissue, and the spotty green tattoos that weave across me like strains of fungus: beneath and between those wretched poultices, I stand white and smooth, resilient and moist, as if I have rolled myself over like a fallen log whose moist underside has been preserved by nutrients from the dirt.

I am stunned by the image of myself as a young man, so perfectly formed I can almost smell the starched, acidic mist rising from his unfurled limbs. His chest heaves in a gesture of surprise traveling down to his groin, and I long to catch the gesture, draw it out into something—anything that will charm him urgently free of his phantomness.

My nipples are rough and distended where they've been pierced. The left is covered by the livid brand of a heart; faint white razor lines spell DEATH TO THE ROTTEN BLOOD SUCKING PUKE LIZARDS (lizards! So that's where they came from) across my rib cage; my chest is slashed beyond legibility and resembles the lacy grafted tissue of a burn victim; I know about the

111

ground glass imbedded in my abdomen, and feel it every time I lean against a counter, but I haven't seen the gravelly skin before; there's a nondescript lump on my thigh where someone has buried a microfilm; my navel has been surgically altered to look like an embossed flower. The colors could be unsettlingly beautiful—plumes of brilliant blue, yellow, orange, red—were they not overwhelmed by the respiring, imperturbable pink of my skin underneath them.

That I have always looked away from myself, averted my eyes whenever I began to see the human contours loom above the shroud of detritus, was perhaps to ward off the precise feeling that is rising through me now: this longing.

I have never seen my plump skin reddened by desire. Had I known of its beauty, I might have risked more to bring this body to exhaustion, and rest.

I don't know if I've labored so long at preventing this love, or creating it. I may be gazing on something I've missed, or I may have taken this long to appreciate it, I can't know: I know only what I see.

Which is not what Stephan sees. What Stephan saw, for the first time, was the permanent record of our association. He shed tears—and was ashamed, perhaps, that his fragile offer of friendship was mocked by the wordless testimony of my body. But Stephan is not fragile himself. Until now, layers of appalling nerve and indifference have enabled him to broker the obsessions of others, moving through them like a man in an asbestos suit. His downfall (and mine) was that he failed to treat me with contempt. He knows that I neither need nor want his pity, but neither do I want a spurious offer of friendship. He might even be rethreading his idea of me now, binding my image to his until we finally become indistinguishable.

I am squinting at this vision through a tattered curtain of black, green, ochre, violet—a hectic, numbing sequence of color made to stop every hour, every minute, and second in its tracks—this curtain of scars is what I've revealed to him.

Revealed to hundreds—I forget—who have seen my flesh in every detail, whose hands have carved and beaten it into its present shape, and whose eyes have all lingered over me, each of them sure that my perfect existence was completely for them! But I am not what I seem. I am like the species of Amazon flower that has learned to bloom in the shape of a female dragonfly. The male insect doesn't know the difference, or pretends not to know, spending his passion without inuring to defeat. All my life I have believed myself an impostor, laboring to bring the shameful seed of deception to term —only to find that camouflage is the latent gene in all possible couplings.

I had forgotten. No, I never even knew, but of course, I have probably been described in hundreds of conversations and letters to magazines, in intimate moments when one lover is persuading another. Someone has described me to Stephan.

What ever gave me the idea that I was saving this knowledge for someone? I've saved it only for myself—I'm the only one who understands—brutally—how to read the cryptic characters. Stephan was mistakenly charmed by what are mere translations of distant rumors, but once seen—my body is gibberish to anyone else.

I cover myself with my robe, and return to the lucid kitchen, full of light.

And the gentle chink of china—

Which is coming from the sliding glass door in the dining room, a contraption opening wide onto the patio. I hear birds, and voices. It's Liann and Stephan, obviously born into the morning light through that gaping hole in the back of my house. They're sitting on the edge of the concrete, warming coffee mugs in their hands, their feet in the unmown grass almost touching.

Their lips move in turns, and I can hear murmurs passing between them. Why hadn't I ever imagined them meeting like this?

I can't make out their words, but the conversation ceases when I step out into the sun. Liann looks up at me, smiling. "Well, look who's up."

Stephan turns away sulkily. Liann casts him an uncertain glance, then gets up and walks by silently on her way back into my eviscerated house.

She returns with the second bottle of Faye's whiskey and stops next to me. She takes a swig, gazing over my poorly concealed limbs, and goes back to her place on the edge of the lawn. I can't help thinking that this is a show, my own back-porch opera—everyone with their assigned seats. Liann pours whiskey into her coffee cup. Her eyes soften briefly, and she tosses me the open bottle.

I bend and catch it, while the spewing whiskey splashes on Stephan's arm, and set it on the ground. I feel wrong, moving about and catching things, when I've become this hideous temple. Disturbed, Stephan is staring at the ground, and now he waits to raise his eyes again. I suppose it's his temple, not hers.

Liann gulps her coffee, and for a moment she is lost in the cup, and I know she's smelling the alcohol evaporate in steam from the hot coffee and that, despite all of this, she is momentarily romanced by it.

Stephan is watching me with real attention, not curiosity and not duty. He isn't going to look at my face, because he can't trust what it says anymore; his eyes are focused on my leg, where the skin is peeking through the folds of cloth, reading it like an historic text. He is trying to discover its chronology, perhaps.

Liann drains her cup. "John, you're a bastard to spring this on me now."

I look at her as squarely as I can.

"I have to go to work," she says. "I have to pick up my mother. If you want a ride, you have exactly five minutes, otherwise you're on your own."

She walks to the door again, hesitates, and puts her hand on my shoulder. I can tell she wants to say something to Stephan, but she can't.

"I'll see you later then."

I was going to answer, but she flicks her hair in front of her face and runs her hand down my back as she goes, so that her fingers are the last to leave.

Stephan stands up. "Do you want me to stop her?" he asks, ready violence in his voice.

I shake my head. We hear the kitchen door slam and her car start up, followed by silence.

I gesture for him to leave, and without looking back, I go to my room, get out of my bathrobe, and dress.

In the living room, he sits with his chin perched on the tips of his woven fingers. "If you want to get away, you can use my room at Physical Culture. I'm hardly ever there."

"Excuse me for a moment." I go into the kitchen, for all appearances to use the phone.

"Hello? This is John. I'm not coming in today. I'm feeling sore from the crash. Yes, I heard. Did they take anything? I'll check tomorrow. See you then."

Stephan is listening in the doorway, the whiskey bottle cradled in his arms.

I shrug. "That's that."

"What are you going to do?" Stephan asks, but there are footsteps on the front porch, and the doorbell is ringing.

"I'll tell her to go away," Stephan says, but halfway across the living room he turns and pushes me back into the kitchen. "It's the police. I saw the car parked out front."

"Go," I say, giving him a shove toward the patio door.

"I'm not the one who broke into a factory," he says, but if Stephan resists me any more, there'll be a scuffle, and I'm certain that getting him out of the house is the most important factor, although now that he's giving in I'm not so sure that my gestures are leading toward anything at all.

Stephan is outside. "I'll be back later," he says, then suddenly laughs. "This is nothing. Don't worry." He takes a reckless hit off the bottle of whiskey, then slinks around the side of the house.

The bell is ringing again.

"Coming. Just a minute," I call, but all I can do is wonder how I came to be moving so fluidly, from one moment to the next, so rapidly that any further thought does nothing but confuse me. There's no sound of feet coming from the front porch, just the sound of a car door closing. I step silently away from the door and go back into the kitchen. All is quiet. Stephan is gone, Liann is gone, and the police are gone. I sit cross-legged on the linoleum floor and lean back against the fridge, staring at the cupboard under the sink, and think about climbing into it for an hour or two, just to break the persistent rushing in my muscles that comes from so much clamorous action. I'm not sure, however, that it would work this time.

The doorbell rings again, and I know without looking that I never heard the squad car drive away. I stand and dust myself off, imagining the number of lapses I will suffer before I emerge on the other side of today, whether I will be capable then of remembering all this correctly.

They are indeed police, I can tell by their clothes, and I'm having an odd sensation of time being wasted as they go ahead and introduce themselves as such. "What is the problem?" I ask.

"Do you work as a bookkeeper at 2511 Foster Road?"

"Yes, I do."

"You're aware, then, that your office was burglarized last night?"

"Yes, I just heard about it." I point to my still bruised face. "I had a car wreck, I'm home resting."

"Apparently, the intruder was surprised by a security guard and fled. We're not sure what the motive was. Has anyone threatened you lately?"

I shake my head, thinking further thoughts.

"Do you owe any money, other than to a legitimate credit establishment?"

"No, of course not. What do you mean?"

"We have reason to believe that someone is trying to disturb you. We came out to ask you some questions about the break-in—what you think they might have been looking for, since nothing was stolen. While we were waiting for you to come to the door, we noticed a man lurking around the side of your house."

I rub the back of my neck and wince. "That must have been the boy who cuts my lawn."

"We don't think so, but would you please come out to the car and identify him?"

I can see Stephan on the far side of the back seat as we approach the car, and I am trying to create the proper response when the cops turn to me.

"Is that your yard boy?" they ask smugly.

Their dull, razor-burnt faces are waiting for me to look again, for a movement of my eyes to show recognition.

"No, that's not him," I say.

"Do you know this man?"

I shake my head.

Stephan looks at me like a stone.

"We have reason to believe he's connected with last night's break-in, so we're taking him in. That whiskey bottle he was carrying is the same brand as the one we found broken in your office this morning. The security guard was hit on the back of the head with it. We'd like you to come in this afternoon and make a statement. If we can't hold him for breaking and entering and assault, you can file charges against him for trespassing. That should hold him overnight, then maybe we can figure out why he's after you."

I nod. "I'll be there as soon as I can."

In a moment they're gone, and from the curb I can hear the phone ringing in my house. I run—up the walkway, up the hollow porch steps, my house hurtling toward me, until I'm inside, in the dim stillness, with the intermittent ringing. I stand in the middle of the kitchen and watch the walls shrink at each shrill, electric clatter. I stand with a dry mouth by the cupboard under the sink, and can't imagine it anymore. I see myself huddled inside there, staring through the vents at Stephan's kneecaps as he comes ranging through the house, to get me. The only thing to do is keep going, see what happens.

And it's Liann on the phone when I answer it. "I need to talk to you," she says, "I'm sorry about the way I acted. I've been thinking, about both of us, and it seems like my drinking, and your—I think we can help each other."

I feel as though I've just awakened from a dream to enter a nightmare, or the other way around. What did I think would happen? Already I can't remember. "Liann, I don't think anybody needs help."

She is silent for a moment. "I was afraid when you didn't answer that you'd gone away. Please don't leave before I see you. You can't just show me what you did last night—then disappear."

I can't think of anything to say. "Yes, alright."

She doesn't believe me. "I've been thinking—"

"Liann," I say, not wanting to hear the rest. "The police just picked up Stephan outside my house. For breaking into the plant."

I hear her gasp.

"He was sneaking around the yard when they caught him. He had that whiskey bottle with him, and they think that he's out to get me. They're positive he's collecting for a loan shark, in fact."

"I'll be right there," she says, then after a pause: "No one will suspect anything, I've been throwing up all morning."

"Don't," I say. "They want me to go down for questioning."

"Shit," Liann says.

"Liann, I stood right there—and said I didn't recognize him." I wanted to say "turned him over," but at the last moment it seemed—vain.

"Jesus."

I can hear her lighting a cigarette then, very businesslike, "Don't leave until I get there," she says.

THURSDAY NIGHT

IT's grown dark outside. I've just emerged on the other side of twilight, watching the shadows of the furniture slip quietly away, then the colors, followed by the interminable pause in which the trees are as flat and gray as my armchair, and the coffee table might be moving among them for all the clues I'm given. Then everything seems to be sketched in granite, so still and opaque, heavy with darkness beneath the freckles of lingering light. I haven't moved, even though the room has sunk into blackness and made possible the pale, vibrant blue images that float and flicker in the air like tropical fish.

I've been waiting, but I don't believe it anymore. I am waiting now just to verify whether or not I've been waiting for something at all. I've become hypnotized by the imminent end of my vigil, which I sometimes expect and more often fear, thinking it will come so suddenly that I will scream out loud. I began waiting for Liann, but she never appeared. Then I

121

waited to go to the police station, but I never went, and then it seemed to me that something must happen, after all, as things have been happening of late, so I sat down to prepare myself.

Perhaps for nothing. Stephan is probably in jail. I will call the station in the morning and tell them not to press charges, then I will collect my things from the office and be done. Liann has simply come to her senses and escaped.

I should be so lucky. I assume now (snapped into alignment by the sound of a car door slamming outside) that Stephan has told the police what he knows about the break-in. The police are knocking on the door for me, and I'm surprised as I cross the carpet that the gestures are the same as if I were going out to check the mail. This is, perhaps, not so different from anything else. I switch on the light as I open the door, to make the room more hospitable.

It's Liann, framed in the light against a shimmer of rain. She kisses me fast on the cheek and walks in, shaking the droplets from her hair, and I feel: I am about to be murdered by relatives who will first demand to be fed. I have never opened my door to someone I know and let them into my house in the evening—but if I told her this, she wouldn't understand what I meant.

"I got him out," Liann says. She perches on the back of the couch and smiles, a bit tremulously. "Let's see if I can remember: He's my boyfriend, and he thought I was messing around with you, so he came around this morning to beat you up and the police saved your poor unsuspecting neck. It's a good thing he was with me last night, or he'd be in trouble, since whoever was in the plant got that bottle of whiskey out of my locker, which happened to be unlocked. It's my opinion that the guard was drinking it when he fell and hit his head, and that, when they found him, he was too scared to admit it. It's not unlikely—since everyone knows I usually have some booze around. And besides—this part is a little silly, but I was making it up as I went along—it's my brand. The police said you couldn't get that brand in this county, which proved my point because I said I had to bring it back from the city, but—why do I get the feeling that nothing I'm saying is making any sense?" Liann stands up.

"The police were about to call you, when the burglary charges were dropped. I don't know why, but I guess we'll hear about it tomorrow. They called the general manager from the station." She winks merrily. "And you don't have to worry about Stephan. He's gone back to where he belongs," she says. "We're going to be alright."

"Liann—" I say, and am shocked by the urgency in my voice.

She takes a forward, anticipatory step.

"I need to have back my truck."

Her lips part. I look down, red-faced.

"Well, alright," she stammers. "I could take you to work in the morning, if you'd like, or—"

"No. I'd just like to get my truck," I say, not without pity. "Please."

Liann nods. "I guess it's best. That way you won't have to—" She doesn't finish, but goes to the phone and calls Eddie. When she comes back, her face is struggling with a fake smile. "You're lucky," she says. "Eddie's already fixed the windshield." She hesitates, attempting to read my expression. She looks like an anthropologist trying to converse with a possible savage. "Shall I drive you there?"

"Yes, thank you," I say quietly. I feel bad that Eddie's done the work, and I ought not to seem so ungrateful.

LATER THURSDAY NIGHT

I RECOGNIZE the boy at the counter doling out towels. He's the one who replaced Stephan.

"Oh, hello," he says in surprise. The phone rings.

"I'd like the key to Stephan's room, please," I say.

He reaches under the counter and brings out the key, handing it to me without comment, then answers the phone, and before he looks back—and before I can think about where I'm going—I've pushed my way through the swinging doors and into a short corridor. I stop and catch my breath.

I'm in the locker room. I recognize a few faces, and we nod, the stiff greeting disposing neatly of any familiarity. I get the feeling that the next time I meet any of these people, even the nod won't be necessary.

Just past the locker room everything is white tile. Each ceramic square has discolored to look like the pink, mucous-like lip of a seashell, as if an oceanful of bony orifices had been laid waste to construct this dank, low-ceiled palace.

Nude men move here and there in misty lassitude, their cheesy, sluggish skin plump with water. Their bodies strike me as squeamish and inept, and one of them—a man about my age with gray, tender skin covered in fine, gray hair—reminds me of a baby bird. He's nodding to his young friend and I'm so afraid that his fragile neck might snap under the next affectionate stroke that I have to look away. It pains me to see this. It sickens me, the responsibility I feel in looking at their nakedness. I remember Stephan, and I'm utterly certain he felt the way I do now. He couldn't help it. He's beautiful and they're pitiful, and I—

Finish it.

Unlike these men, I am fully clothed. I thought I was concealing something. Really I was just refusing to look at *them*.

Physical Culture. Is it a mold—that disgusts people simply because it's so small and parasitic? Or is it a primitive culture—the noble savages and all that? No, it isn't either of those. Physical Culture is culture in the operatic sense: it's drama and fiction and tragedy taken to a maudlin extreme, it's pretense and miniscule, futile omniscience, complete with stage blood and fat divas. Physical Culture, the art of body building—the willful distortion of muscle tissue to imitate the extremes suggested by real life—is bulging blood-and-guts opera.

For me, it was vanity: they were actors, moving through a useless plot, and I was authentic. I was the one who concocted them a legend.

Through a pane of glass I can see a willful couple spotting each other on free-weights. They look like animated mannequins, and I go on, through the door that says STAIRWELL—EXIT, and up.

Now I'm on Stephan's side, behind the scenes.

Most of the doors are hanging wide open. The empty rooms may have been offices once for small, single-desk businesses. Somewhere I hear voices. I know Stephan's room faces off the street, and the key in my hand fits a padlocked door at the end of the hall.

I switch on the light. The landlord's halo shudders on and off, then admits the tiny, yellow-walled room to view. The thin, bland light still seems to be harboring darkness, trembling at the possibility of sudden exposure. An orange drafting lamp is screwed to the edge of the nightstand, and I exchange its direct beam for the other.

The room is half in shadow, and I can tell that it's more comfortable that way. There is so little here—a chair, a bed, a night table, a hall tree draped in clothing. I'm sitting lightly on the edge of a narrow bed. The sheets are crumpled and slightly gritty under my hand. If I put my nose to them, I'll know how recently he's slept here—but instead I hook my finger through the handle of the only drawer in the nightstand and pull. A tabloid that's been lying doubled over slowly unfurls itself. It's just a week old. Underneath it—a packet of tissues, a jar of petroleum jelly, a bottle of aspirin, toenail clippers, empty matchbooks, a disposable razor, a tube of antifungal creme, and in the back of the drawer, there is something leathery, soft, and weighty, with the size and heft of a scrotum.

It's a sap. I hold it lightly by the neck and slap it into my cupped palm. It fits there, feels natural and safe. The luxurious leather tissue, the easy fit, make the gentle slapping gesture irresistible.

These are the things that Stephan uses to maintain and protect himself.

I return the sap to the drawer and take out the aspirin bottle, shaking half of its contents onto the table. All the pills are not the same size and shape. Which interrupts my tenderness with disappointment.

Until I catch sight of the white towel hanging on the back of his door and am reminded of Stephan's nakedness, the impermeability, the endlessness of his skin, how familiar it must be to him, how great a burden it is to live under the spell and unspoken power of beauty, to refrain, as always in deference to one's beauty, from inventing oneself fully—and to resist the gesture hidden in the shape of the sap.

I scoop the pills back into the bottle and close the drawer.

There's a knock on the door.

"Come in."

The young man from downstairs stands in the doorway. He's about Stephan's age, shirtless, in light blue trousers, his cropped hair curling in the humidity.

"Can I get you anything?" he asks, his hand poised on the doorknob.

The knowledge I have of the sap and the pills and the nail clippers burns like a secret, or a common, unacknowledged truth. I lay my hand on the table where the objects are concealed, but it is cool to the touch, and reassuring. The boy probably knows his way around Stephan's room as if it were his own. He might use this room, too—to look at him.

Yes, I'm having trouble conjuring Stephan's face: the two of them are interchangeable at the moment.

"No," I say, quietly, politely. "Thank you, I'm fine."

The boy smiles broadly. "Stephan told me that when you came—"

I don't want him to go. In Physical Culture he's a welcome sight.

"It's alright," I say, hesitantly. "But if you could bring me a towel."

"Right." He's gone.

I remove my shirt, then shoes, socks, and trousers, leave them all neatly arranged on a chair, and climb into Stephan's bed, stretching out under the white sheet, my head and arms free. I open the drawer again and leave it slightly ajar, so that in his absence, Stephan's things can bear witness.

The boy comes back with the towel and, seeing me, closes the door behind him. He sits on the edge of the bed and touches my arm.

"You have to tell me what you would like," I say softly.

He smiles and laughs, but not in derision.

"It's very important for *you* to decide," I repeat.

I can tell that he's trying to think of the right answer, the way his eyes are making brief references to the surface of my arms, the way the touch of his fingers is so indecisive. This is a waste of time, perhaps. He is much too affected by my presence.

Poor Stephan, I think, alone in this dingy yellow room with his bottle of pills and his toenail clippers. I might never have thought of it.

The boy must have seen the drift in my attention, because

he awkwardly gestures for me to turn over. I'm looking now at the wall, my cheek against the creased sheet. I hear him standing, undressing, and feel the bed move as he climbs over me.

I feel too aware of myself, and my muscles keep tensing in anticipation of his touch, until his knee brushes against my thigh and I can suddenly imagine him there, can feel him shifting his weight, and hear wood against wood—I rear up and grab his wrist as it plunges into the drawer.

But he's stronger than I am and pushes me down, first with a hand between my shoulder blades, and then with all his weight. His hand, heedless of the grip I have on his wrist, emerges from the drawer with the jar of petroleum jelly.

I burst out laughing.

He rises above me, as if the unexpected heaving of my lungs has blown him into the air. I roll onto my back and grin at him stupidly.

He sits in naked amazement, the jar of grease in his limp hand.

"I'm sorry," I say, flustered. "This is ridiculous. Give me that."

He hands over the jar.

I return it to the drawer, take the sap, and close his fingers around its stem, keeping it in his hand with both of mine.

"What I want," I say, "is for you to hit me with this. Once, quickly, somewhere to draw blood."

He doesn't appear to comprehend.

"Only once, understand? What you see"—I glance at my own chest—"isn't your problem. I just want you to do this one thing for me."

I let go of his hands.

He shakes his head somewhere between bewilderment and refusal. "I'm sorry, no. I can't do that."

He is, I know, much too strong for me, but I grab hold of his wrist once more. "I'm not asking you to do anything else. Just one good rap. It has nothing to do with you."

"I won't," he says, keeping calm. He glances at his entrapped wrist. "There's a limit, see."

"You're here, aren't you?" I say coldly. "What are you going to do about it?"

He begins to stand, but I pull him down again, more through desperation than strength. I'll try another tactic.

"Stephan told you to take care of me, didn't he?" I say, and I mean it as an accusation. I keep forgetting how I appear to him.

He shifts only his eyes away this time. I can tell he's afraid of me. "Stephan hardly comes here anymore. I don't know where he is."

"Look," I say, "don't be stupid about this. It's not as if I'm asking you to cut me to ribbons."

He's looking at my body again, as if he hadn't seen it the first time or hadn't known what to think.

"I'll send someone up," he mutters lamely, attempting to rise.

"No. It has to be you."

"Let me go," he says, "I don't do that kind of thing."

"Come on, get it over with," I say bitterly, thinking that I'm not looking forward to this any more than he.

"Please! Let go of my hand."

"No one's asked you to like it."

He stands abruptly, and I realize that I'm not about to let him go. I may not be able to do anything else, but I can at least hold onto his wrist for as long as necessary. Surely he'll stop short of dragging me all the way through the steam room.

"Stop it!"

He's surprised to find my weight attached to him. We're standing now, and he's lurching toward the door and I'm dragging my feet and pulling at him. It must look awful.

I swing around so that my back slams up against the door and he is spinning around to face me.

There we are.

He doesn't know whether to be terrified or annoyed, and I'm tired of pulling at him.

"You stupid little bastard," I say, and kick him fiercely in the shin.

It can't have hurt him much, with my bare foot, but I think that the shock of assault is doing the trick. He still holds the sap in his free hand and swings it in panic.

My forearm burns as if a fat snake has burrowed under my skin.

The sap lands again and again, until I feel a vent of heat emerge somewhere from the humps of pain. I curl my arms around my body and lurch toward the bed.

"Are we even now?" I spit between gasps.

The boy drops the sap on the ground and swears, then he is over me, two hands light as birds on my shoulders, helping me down. I fall forward, clinging to myself, curling up small and tight. He says nothing.

132

I squeeze his hand, as if it means anything to him, then wave him away. He vacillates for a long time, and I can hear him growing still, withdrawing.

My hipbone is the source of heat. I know all about this, don't I? For a moment, despite myself, I feel peaceful in a place I know I'm not supposed to go.

Then I ignore it, rise, and sit with my head between my hands. The skin over my hipbone has split apart, and runs thickly with blood. Stephan's sheets are bloody where I've lain. This is, after all, what I meant.

"Don't change the sheets," I say, and reach for my clothes.

The boy is bewildered. There are tears of awakening shame in his eyes.

F R I D A Y

I'M driving to the office in my truck, which has a new windshield. I don't like the new windshield, because somehow I feel that the scar of my behavior has fled from the glass to me. I can't locate it, but I can feel its weight, the fact that I'm left with only a memory to sustain the events of the past few days. How did I crash the truck? I must have been dreaming. There must be a way, and I'll find it, to take these things out and examine them. But already I feel this sequence of time dissolving into my bloodstream. If I could speak of what's happened, it would dry, harden, crust over in contact with the air, or simply bleed to death.

I am also trying to make sense of the things I have already said—to others. The project leaves a bad taste in my glands and makes me shudder. On the other hand, I'm excited by this peculiar melancholy, about as disturbing as a set of paisley curtains billowing in the wind, which is not to say that it is anything slight at all. The most destructive, sapping fears come and go so quickly they sometimes feel like malaise. I will discover, by memory or revelation, the toll I have exacted, and might, if my worst fears are founded, learn some horrible truth each day and forget it by the next, experiencing in those spaces of terror a moment or two of awareness, however deformed and inviable.

I am three blocks from her house right now, and if I could see her, I would cease to believe in my own powers and begin, simply, to abide in confusion. It's amazing, if you think about it, how little of anything actually determines our next move and how well that fact is suppressed.

I haven't turned where I should to pick up Marjorie, or even thought about her with a trace of positive intention. I've pretty much written Marjorie off, and I have no idea whether she's dead or alive, or whether her present condition has anything to do with me.

I'm not picking up Marjorie for one reason: Liann and Stephan have met, converged, and the opera is over. My tongue is heavy and silver with electricity at the thought, and I think it might curl back compulsively to clog my throat—a mute, frustrating response, for I cannot discern an emotion in its company. I am more shocked than afraid, more curious than knowledgeable, but I could be wrong. It's a feeling that already—I'm watching it go—will leave me with nothing but a handful of wasted jism. To pick up Marjorie in the midst of this would be positively four-dimensional.

Besides, I'm retiring. I will enjoy a new kind of chaos that seems inevitable now. It will not cost me the same as my rational pleasures did, but I will no longer have the luxury of believing my misery is personal. As mistaken as I might have been, I believed myself to be bleeding inside the belly of life. However, just at this moment—I'm having trouble remembering what I thought, whether I lived there or merely longed for it. I'm too traumatized to care, although I know if I did, I'd despair at the vacuous world—the sheer volume of air and movement one must consume to live through it.

Yet I must also believe that all is right with the pavement and strips of grass—things I once remember as intimate, on a close, rainy day when I was soaked and cold and could not object. Soon I will be conscious again, walking between rows of parked cars. But that day in the rain may leap into my mind once again. I don't know. I might—in a blind, catastrophic moment—stab a pencil through my wrist when I'm alone in my living room. Liann and Stephan, I was thinking about them a minute ago, had constructed something, but now I seem to have abandoned that theory.

I'm early, and the parking lot is only half-full. I park far away so I can walk as fast as I want to. Marjorie would be gasping in the gravel by now, some twenty feet behind me, as I run up the stairs. The receptionist gives me a special smile, the kind saved for weddings and funerals: it's Friday, my last day. I smile back as esoterically as I can, and frighten her when I reach into her wastepaper basket for a cardboard box.

Down the hallway.

"John! John." The general manager darts out of his office and accompanies me down the hall. He looks red in the face. "John, I think, given the circumstances, you can just pick up today and leave whenever you want. Don't worry about getting any work done. You've had a rough week."

He seems to be apologizing for something he's about to tell me. "To be honest, I've already had a service come in to do the books. Would you come into my office for a moment?"

I follow him, smile to myself, and sit down in his comfortable chair, looking at him from across the desk. It strikes me for the first time that I don't like this man. I try to have no expression.

He purses his fat lips. "Listen, John. I have a couple of things to say." He decides to close the door instead of sitting down, as a preface. I can see he doesn't know where to go, so he sits on the edge of his desk. "I know sometimes a guy hits retirement and thinks he needs to prove something. And you're younger than usual, so it's harder for you. I don't want to intrude, but this has become my business. Let's just call it friendly advice, alright?"

I nod once, annoyed that he's made me accept this "advice" before hearing it.

"John, in short: that girl is trouble for you. I dropped the charges as soon as I figured out that it was probably her and her boyfriend who were in here Wednesday night—the guy they caught at your house. I like her mother and I didn't want to see Marjorie hurt. I'm doing you a favor, keeping your name out of it, too." His cupped hands almost meet, then fall to cover his knees.

I can't be bothered with pretending I don't know what he's talking about, and I'm actually tempted to ask him how it matters. However, he seems to have taken possession of the event, from the way his hands held it a moment ago—and he must be pretty sure of his authority to leave it hanging there in front of him. The whole incident seems to mean less, at least to me, now that he's claimed it for himself.

He goes on: "I let her go this morning. I've been looking for a reason to fire her ever since she came back. She's a boozer. Do you remember the time she got her finger sliced in the hopper? The insurance company told me to ignore it that time, but I've been watching her closely. If I hadn't, I might not have put two and two together, but anyway. Just don't fall prey to her shit. She's a lush, and what's more, she's caused trouble by sleeping around with every guy on the line. *And* the office. She can't keep her personal life out of the workplace, and that makes her disruptive and dangerous. We're talking heavy machinery here, and it's no joke. You've had a difficult week and I don't blame you for your weaknesses, but you're not the first with her."

I shrug, almost imperceptibly.

He wipes his palms together and glances at me briefly. "No hard feelings, understand. You've been Johnny-on-the-spot for twenty-five years. This is no time to start anything with you."

I nod.

"As I said, you can leave whenever you want." He stands and extends a hand. "John," he says formally, "it's been a pleasure."

I shake the hand. "Likewise."

He closes the door to his office behind me, and I'm glad, because I want to walk slowly down the hall to my own little cell, so I'll be ready for it.

I look at the things on my desk. A coffee mug full of pens. A magnet crawling with paper clips. An electric pencil sharpener. Come to think of it, I'm not sure if any of it belongs to me. There's a stack of expediting notes in a folder between two bookends. No one else could read them, so I put them in the trash. It's kind of silly to come here just to do that, so I toss the assorted pens in the garbage as well. My replacement will have to bring his own. The calendar on the wall has my scribbles on it, too, so I toss that. There isn't anything I want to put in the box. The only thing I'll miss is the check-writing machine, but I can't take that. I go through the files, pulling out anything that catches my eye and junking it. There's a framed photograph of a skier on the wall that I've always hated, so I think I'll throw that out, too, out of mercy.

I seem to be done. I've thrown away a lot of things that aren't mine, and that's about it. It's sort of similar to swabbing down a nasty cubicle—the nastiness is still there, but it's probably my own fault. It's taken me twenty-five years to make this cubicle disgusting, and I feel as if I'm bound to leave some shred of evidence behind. I'm glad I brought the box. There's nothing to put in it, but I'm closing the flaps anyway, and I'll heft it against my hip as if it contained the usual sentimental excrement. I wouldn't want anyone to think I wasn't taking care of business.

The doors in the hall are mostly closed as I leave, I believe out of shyness. These people who never knew me do not know how to bid me farewell, a thing I find touching. I can hear their hearts wince as I walk past their doors with my wretched cardboard box. The receptionist is on the phone, so she's happy to flash me a slightly muddled smile as I walk out. The last thing I hear is the growling respiration of machinery, grunting, it seems, under the effort to squeeze me out the door. I go. But I'm sly, I think: I've managed, at the very last minute, to feel desire.

PERHAPS the cries of pain would save me the groans of unhappiness, and the lacerations of my body would prevent that of my heart.

—*J.J. Rousseau*